"So this is good-bye," I said sadly.

He held out his hand. "You're a delightful girl, Kelly, and I know things will come out right for you."

I was too choked up to say anything. Instead of shaking his hand, I put my arms around him and hugged him. He seemed surprised, but then he hugged me back and kissed my cheek. I raced back to Grandmother's. Love and support, he had said. The most important thing is love and support. The words flew inside me like banners in the wind.

THE SHELL
LADY'S
DAUGHTER

C. S. Adler

FAWCETT JUNIPER • NEW YORK

Acknowledgment
The author is grateful to Susan Britain,
Ph.D. in Psychology, of Clifton Park, New York.
Her generous contribution of knowledge and experience
added to and helped refine this book.

RLI: $\dfrac{\text{VL: } 6 + \text{up}}{\text{IL: } 7 + \text{up}}$

A Fawcett Juniper Book
Published by Ballantine Books

Library of Congress Catalog Card Number: 82-19801

ISBN 0-449-70095-X

This edition published by arrangement with Coward-McCann, Inc.

Manufactured in the United States of America

First Ballantine Books Edition: December 1984

To Lauren Beth Adler,
The first of the next generation. Salutations,
blessings and much love.

Chapter 1

I had promised my mother we'd go shopping that Saturday in March, just the two of us the way it used to be, but Jennifer called and invited me to her house. When she told me who was going to be there, I didn't hesitate to say I'd come. Then I went to ask Mother if she minded putting off our trip.

Mother was already dressed for it in her blue blazer, plaid skirt and high-heeled pumps. She stood at the old oak desk, recently bought at a garage sale, searching through the million and one drawers and mumbling about where she'd stuck that receipt.

"All set for our big date, sweetheart?" she asked when I said good morning. Her vivid smile increased my guilt. For the past year I've spent most of my free time with Jennifer and neglected Mother. I knew that she'd been looking forward to today.

"Jennifer just called," I said. Mother's smile hung on gamely, though I could tell she knew what was coming. "She said Mark is coming over to practice for his performance at the coffee house tonight—his parents won't let him practice at home—and he's bringing Troy Astemborski to work with him."

"Is Troy Astemborski somebody special?"

"He's that boy who stopped me in the hall and asked for my autograph. Remember?"

"Oh yes, the one who said you looked like a movie star." Mother's eyebrows went up as her smile came down and her pert face changed from happy to quizzical. My mother's got the most expressive face. Her tip-tilted nose is cute, and she's funny and pretty at the same time, but that Saturday I wished I couldn't see what she was thinking.

"I know it's a line," I said. "But the thing is he noticed me and Troy's the cutest boy in the whole junior class."

"Lots of boys will be noticing you, Kelly."

"Please, mother, would you mind if we put our date off till next weekend?"

"Well, I mind," she said, "and I don't know if it's such a hot idea for you to be running around with juniors when you're a newly hatched freshman . . ."

"You don't think I'm mature enough to take care of myself?"

"Oh, I know you're mature, my darling. You've been a little adult ever since you were three years old, but you're only fourteen and this boy—"

"I'm just going to Jennifer's house, Mother, not out on a date with him."

She nodded and turned to fuss with some papers at the other side of the desk so I couldn't see her expression. "Okay," she said. "Have fun, but be careful."

"I will. Thanks." I hugged her. When she kissed

me, I saw that she looked close to tears. "Mother, if you really want me to stay with you . . ."

"No, no, darling. You go ahead. I'll be fine. Do I look funny? Don't worry about that. I'm probably just coming down with a cold or something. You go to Jennifer's."

I felt so guilty about standing Mother up that I nearly changed my mind, but it was already too late to save her feelings, and I didn't want to miss what might be my one chance with Troy.

Mother had always said I'm her best friend. It used to make me proud when she said that. Other girls complain that their mothers nag them and won't let them make their own decisions. My mother discusses everything with me. She's treated me like an adult since I was practically an infant. It's partly because I'm an only child, I guess, and because my father is away from home for months at a time. He's a pilot for a family corporation with businesses all over the world. He has to wait around foreign airports ready to fly his bosses wherever and whenever they want to go. I've been my mother's companion at Saturday night movies and ballets and fancy restaurants. I've attended receptions for artists at museum show openings where I was the lone child present. Sometimes it was boring. Mostly it made me feel special. But now I have finally found a good friend my own age, and boys are beginning to notice me. The truth is, lately it's begun to scare me that I'm my mother's best friend. Not that I don't still love her and think she's the warmest, most wonderful mother in the world, but I don't plan to spend the rest of my life with her. Kids are supposed to go away to college and leave home to get married, aren't they? Maybe it's selfish of me to be pulling away, but she does have my father and I'm only going to be young once.

I spent the afternoon with Jennifer in her family room listening to the boys practice their numbers on guitars. Troy made up a song just for me, at least he said it was. It went:

Shy girl, don't run away.
Come steal your arms around me,
Slip into my heart, surround me
*   with your wings of hair.*
Shy girl, I have not lost my heart to bolder,
Wouldn't kiss the lips of older
*   if you were there.*
Shy girl, wish you were my girl, shy girl.

"Well?" he asked me when he'd finished singing.

"But I'm not shy," I said like an idiot instead of telling him I liked his song. I guess he didn't mind because he walked me home anyway. It was already dark, beginning to snow, and much later than Mother expected me back.

"Aren't you going to thank me for the song?" Troy asked while I fumbled for the key to our hundred-and-fifty-year-old Colonial, the only really old house in the development surrounding us.

"Sure," I said. He gave me the wickedest grin and then he kissed me. It was my first kiss. My heart flip-flopped and I rushed into the house to tell Mother all about it. I found her in the den. She was sitting in the armchair in the moonglow cast by the jug lamp with the accordion-pleated shade. She had her needlepoint in her lap and the television on very low. The needlepoint was a kind of joke. Mother called it her lifework because she'd been at it off and on for years, making pale green seat covers each decorated with a wreath of flowers for our dining room chairs.

"Mother," I said. "Do you mind if I turn the TV off? I've got to tell you what happened today. . . . Mother?" She wasn't looking at me. Her eyes were on her needlework, but she didn't seem to be doing anything with it, and then I looked at her hands. Even in that dim lamplight, I could see the little drops of blood all over her left palm. I gasped and went down on my knees beside her and asked what had happened. She looked at me so blankly, her eyes wide and spacy. "Mother? What's the matter with you?"

Finally she said, "Kelly, I'm not feeling too well. I think I'd better go to bed." She stood and I picked up the needlepoint canvas. It was all smeared with blood. I didn't know what to do. My father was in San Juan. I followed Mother to the bathroom and made sure she was all right. She went about getting ready for bed in her regular way. I waited until she was safely in bed, kissed her good night and wrapped a clean rag around her hand, which was still oozing a little blood.

"What's that for?" she asked me.

"To keep the blood off the sheets," I said.

"Oh," she said as if that were not unusual. She closed her eyes and I ran to call my father. We always keep the telephone number of his hotel handy above the wall phone in the kitchen. He wasn't in his room, but I left a message that he should please call home, that his daughter had to speak to him urgently. Luckily, I answered when he called early Sunday morning. He wasn't due home for another week, but I told him something seemed to be wrong with Mother; so he switched times off with his partner and got home Sunday afternoon. By then Mother was acting fine. She sparkled for him almost as much as usual, asking, "What are you doing home, honey? Don't tell me. It's such a lovely surprise. How long do we get to keep you? Are you hungry? Kelly, go get a steak from the freezer." She had disappeared the bloody needlepoint somewhere, thrown it away, I guess. When Dad started hinting around about her hand, she put him off and wouldn't show it to him and teased and fooled around and sat on his lap and cuddled with him. Before long she got him talking about the trip he'd just made to the Canary Islands and how the control tower got them all fouled up and they'd narrowly avoided landing in the ocean. Dad seems to like flying best when there's a challenge in it, but that's okay because Mother doesn't worry about him. She's convinced herself that he leads a charmed life.

The next day I asked my father if he'd seen Mother's hand yet. He said he didn't think it was anything serious. She seemed fine to him. By Monday afternoon he was gone. It's not that Dad doesn't care, it's just that anything to do with emotions never seems real to him. He's low keyed, controlled and steady, a sort of foundation person while mother is the decorative trim. He'd have had to see that needlepoint himself to be convinced something was wrong.

For a while after that, I watched Mother carefully, but she seemed to be her old enthusiastic self, always involved in a project, which she usually abandoned halfway through. Our house is filled with used furniture Mother's picked up at auctions and garage sales. She has great plans for repairing and refinishing everything—eventually—when she gets around to it. Dad and I tease her about her halfway done projects. Other kids' mothers have a career, and sometimes I've thought that's what Mother needs, but the closest she's come is collecting a pile of credits toward a fine arts degree and taking part-time jobs occasionally. I think she has a lot of artistic talent and could have a career if she wanted one, but she says she needs her time free to spend with my father on the odd weeks when he gets off, although all he does when he's home is lie around reading spy stories or fix things around the house. Mother's other excuse for not sticking to anything is that she isn't good enough. Actually, she's good at a lot of things, cooking for instance. She makes delicious quiches and fattening desserts, but just for me and Dad because we're built slim and never put on weight. Mother's always dieting. Not that she's fat, just rounded and soft. The friends she's made have mostly been from weight-watching groups or exercise classes. She was big on aerobics for a while. I don't know why her friends never seem to last. People like her, but she claims to like people best in groups. "That way you don't begin to depend on them and they can't disappoint you," she says. I don't agree with Mother. I've always wished I had a close friend. Jennifer means a lot to me.

Sometimes this spring when I got home from school, Mother would be waiting for me in the garden, cleaning the dead winter leaves out of the flower beds or fertilizing them, but often she'd be napping. She spent an awful lot of time sleeping.

She stopped getting up to see me off to school in the mornings too, not that I minded, but still . . . She used to be a night owl, staying up to watch the late late show on television, but this spring she began going to bed early, especially if I was doing something with Jennifer. Mother wasn't sick. At least, I don't think she was. Once when she looked pale, I asked her if she felt all right and she said, "Sometimes I feel as if my skin's crawling. It's the most awful sensation. I want to tear it off me."

"You should see a doctor, Mother," I said. "Maybe you're allergic to something."

"I've been to the doctor. He says I'm fine."

"Well, go see another one. Something must be wrong with you."

"I'm fine. I'm just fine, darling. Tell me, what's new with Jennifer?" And she smiled her lovely smile and listened to me, her pert face all attention.

I did blow it another time that I remember. My conscience had been bothering me, as usual, because I wasn't spending time with Mother; so I asked her to go on a bike hike, "Just you and me this Saturday."

"Oh, that would be fun, Kelly," she said enthusiastically. "I'll get my old bike out. I haven't ridden it in a dog's age. Maybe I'd better ride around the neighborhood a few times. Your poor old mom is gonna have to get in shape to keep up with you."

I encouraged her. Our Colonial is in a hilly area surrounded by a development with houses on half-acre lots. The only way you can tell them apart is by the color of their shutters, but big old trees make the area look pretty anyway, trees and the hills and curves. On Friday, Mother claimed she'd conquered every hill around. She was so pleased that I was glad I'd suggested the bike hike.

But then Friday afternoon, Jennifer walked home with me after school and asked what I was doing Saturday. I couldn't thing of how to say no to her when she invited herself along. "I like your mother so much," she said.

We were going to eat down at the railroad station picnic area. Mother and I made a lunch big enough to feed the three of us. She didn't act disappointed that Jennifer was coming too. We set off early on a gorgeous spring day full of robins and pale green leaves. Mother is not the greatest athlete, so she soon fell behind. Jennifer and I tried to slow down. Actually, Mother did well on the flat parts of the bike path. She kept exclaiming about what a pretty day it was and did we see that cardinal. Nobody gets as much fun out of little things as my mother. I thought she was doing fine and stopped worrying about leaving her behind as I rode alongside Jennifer and listened to the latest episode of her romance with Mark. When I finally looked back and saw that Mother wasn't even in sight, Jennifer and I stopped to wait for her. Half an hour later, we backtracked to find her. She was sitting on a fence rail staring at the river, which ran close to the path right there.

"Mother, are you all right?"

"I'm okay, just not the bike rider I thought I was. Why don't you girls go ahead and I'll meet you back at the picnic table at the lock for lunch." Her voice was flat, but her smile was on.

Even so, I said, "That's not fair. We were going to do this together. Why don't we all have lunch now and then go home."

"On this glorious day? It's perfect for bike riding. No, I insist," Mother said. "You kids enjoy yourselves. I'll be fine here, believe me. If you could feel the way my calf muscles are acting up, you'd know how fine I'll be just sitting." She made a funny face to mock herself.

I thought she meant it, or I let myself believe she meant it, because it was a beautiful day, and, like my father, I get a high from exercise. Well, I left her. There was nothing else special about that day. I don't know why I remember it so well.

On my dresser I have a wicker shelf where I keep small things that matter to me. Next to the cut-glass salt shaker where I stow the blue jay feathers is a tulip shell. It looks sort of like a whelk and has an orange pencil stripe spiraling around its tan-and-white body. It's one of the prettiest shells I ever found on the beach. Mother and I found it together. We were making the only visit I ever made to my grandparents, who live on the east coast of Florida. They're my father's parents. We don't see much of them. Mother's always blamed time and distance when I ask her about that, but I wonder. I can remember her calling my grandmother "the Queen Mother" when she thought I wasn't listening. She said to my father, "The Queen Mother says they can't make it—again. She suggests we visit them when they return from the Orient, but she didn't mention when that would be."

I was eight the Christmas week Mother and I spent at my grandparents' house. I remember that when we found the tulip shell, Mother made up a shell lady story. It might have been the first one. There have been several over the years. I know them all by heart. The first one went like this:

Once a little goose girl, watching her geese in a village hidden in the mountains of a far-off land, found a handsome prince asleep near the stream where her geese swam. He looked so cold that the goose girl pitied him and covered him with her own winter coat. When the prince awoke, he was so grateful for her kindness that he asked her to marry him. Well, the goose girl couldn't believe her good fortune, since she had already fallen in love with the handsome prince, but they were married in the village, to the envy of all the other girls.

The prince took the goose girl to live in a castle in the middle of an empty plain. Every day she sat waiting for him while he rode out on his horse to do great deeds, and every night when he returned, she covered him with goose-down quilts to warm him. They were happy until one day the prince took the goose girl to visit his father, who was a great king on an island with many strange customs. The great king was scornful of the simple girl his son had married.

"Can she weave tapestries of spiders' webs? Can she sing flute songs that float on the winds? Can she do anything?"

"She covers me with quilts at night to keep me warm," the prince said. His father laughed and the prince was shamed. He didn't know anymore why he had married the goose girl, and he turned his eyes away from her and left her alone on the island. Then she had no one to cover with quilts at night when it was cold. She had no one at all. She would have died, but the king of the sea felt sorry for her and caught her dying spirit to set it in a tulip shell where she could live forever while she waited for her prince to return.

* * *

All Mother's shell lady stories were sad. Sometimes they made me cry, because she looked so
serious as she told them that they seemed real. But
as soon as she finished a sad tale, Mother would
suggest something that was fun. It used to be,
"Want to dance with me, Kelly?" She'd put music on
the tape deck and we'd tap dance around our
asphalt-tiled playroom doing all the combinations
we learned at tap and ballet lessons when I was ten.
Or she'd suggest we make fudge, or if it was
springtime, go into the woods behind our house to
see if the lady's slippers had returned. Parties were
what Mother did best. At the start of school, she'd
let me invite as many classmates as I liked. She'd
make quilted pocketbooks as favors and funny
newspaper hats. On Halloween she'd dress up as a
witch to go trick-or-treating with me. She really
seemed to like little kids and they liked her back.

It could be the best thing Mother did for me was
act as if I was wonderful. She knew I had faults, but
she didn't dwell on them. Instead, she told me how
capable I was, and athletic, and intelligent and
beautiful besides. Luckily, I knew my own weak-
nesses. Like being too self-centered and judging
people too much instead of just accepting them as
they are, the way I would if I were a really sweet
person like Jennifer. Also, I was awkward with
people my own age. And lately, though it embarrassed me to admit it, all I thought about most of
the time was boys. The truth was I was not a
faithful best friend to my mother anymore, not
even a very good daughter.

Chapter 2

In June I finally gave up on Troy even though he occasionally did me the honor of winking when he passed me in the halls at school.

"Forget Troy. He made up with his old girl friend," Jennifer said. "Listen, Kelly, Mark's bringing his cousin over this weekend. He's cute. Just don't tell him how old you are, okay?"

"But Mark will tell him, won't he?" I asked.

"I told him not to," Jennifer said.

"You always say my age doesn't matter."

"It doesn't, except to some people it might."

"Fourteen isn't that much younger than sixteen," I argued.

"Mark's cousin is seventeen. Listen, it's not going to kill you to keep quiet about your age. He'll only be here for the Memorial Day weekend."

Mark's cousin, Gerry, was so handsome he made me shiver. We ended up back at Jennifer's house after we'd played tennis in the park together, all four of us. We had a spaghetti supper, and then

Gerry asked about the old tree house in the enormous maple in Jennifer's backyard.

"Nobody but my little brother has used it for years," Jennifer said.

"Wanna go see how the moon looks through the leaves, Kelly?" Gerry asked me.

I knew when I said yes what I was getting myself into. No way to plead innocent. I knew, but I went anyway. The only thing I hadn't realized was how fast he would move. One minute we were like little kids, climbing up the rickety crossbars nailed to the tree into the shaky platform and gawking together at the stars through the spaces between the branches, grasping each other's hand and whispering in the darkness. The next minute his lips came down on mine. The soft wetness of his open mouth surprised me and the probing of his tongue felt weird.

"Hey," I whispered, pulling back. "Hey!" I couldn't tell him I'd only been kissed once in my life. Then he started pouring words over me, how pretty I was, how sexy, graceful as a wood nymph and mysterious. While he was mesmerizing me with words, his fingers were sketching a line from my ear down the side of my neck to my chest. An icy tickle of delight followed the path of his finger. I was struck dumb that the touch of a seventeen-year-old boy I'd just met could do that to me.

When he started unbuttoning my blouse, I said, "But, we don't even know each other."

"This is how we'll get to know each other faster," he said. He was pulling the blouse from my shoulders and murmuring something about the whiteness of my skin in the moonlight. I got scared.

I didn't know how to stop him. If I jumped from the tree house, I'd break a leg.

"Listen," I said, tossing it at him like a water balloon, "I'm only fourteen years old."

He stopped. Then he questioned me. When he finally believed me, he was angry. He thought he'd been tricked. All of a sudden I wasn't a wood nymph but a rotten little tease. He climbed down the tree first. I followed slowly, my legs almost too weak to bear my weight. At the botton, I straightened my clothes, and without going back to Jennifer's house to wait for her father to escort me, I walked the six blocks home. I wanted to spill it all out to Mother. I wanted her to comfort me.

When I got home, the house was lit upstairs and down. My father's car was in the driveway and behind his, another car. I hadn't expected to see my father. I certainly didn't expect to see the doctor, who was standing in the living room talking to him.

"Kelly, thank God you're here! I was just about to call the police," my father said.

"Call the police? What for? I was just over at Jennifer's. Mother knows that."

"Your mother's taken sick. The doctor wants to put her in the hospital."

"You're kidding," I protested. "She was all right this morning. She was still in bed when I left her. She's been tired a lot lately so she stays in bed. Probably she reads too much at night so she gets tired, but she was all right. She knew I wouldn't be home until late. I told her where I was going and she . . ." I stopped babbling. I had been about to say, "and she didn't say a word," but that in itself was strange. Mother should have said, "Don't be home late," or "If Jennifer's folks can't bring you home, call me and I'll come get you," or "Why don't you bring Jennifer over here for supper?" But she hadn't said any of those motherly sounding things.

"What is she sick with?" I asked.

"We don't know," my father said.

Then the doctor began quizzing me. How long had Mother been sleeping so late in the mornings? How long had she been acting "down"? How long? I didn't know. This new doctor of mother's had a baby face. He didn't look any smarter than the others she had tried and discarded. What could he know about her? Was my mother mentally ill? Not my mother, not my warm, lively, fun-loving mother.

"How come you're home, Dad? Did the doctor call you?" I asked when the doctor had gone back upstairs to his patient.

"No, I called him when I found your mother. Didn't she tell you I was due home tonight?"

"She didn't say a word."

He squeezed my shoulder as if to give me courage and said, "Kelly, would you make me a cup of coffee? I could use a plate of soup or something too. I'm going to help get her settled in the hospital, and when I come home, I'd appreciate something to eat. Okay?"

"Sure," I said. "But first I want to see Mother."

"No, not a good idea. You stay in the kitchen."

"But Dad, I have to see Mother."

"Listen, Kelly," he said. "I know how you feel, but the doctor doesn't think it would be a good idea for you to see her now."

"Why? She's my mother." I raised my voice. "She's *my* mother."

The shriek of an ambulance cut off my plea. I froze as it stopped in our driveway. "Stay in the kitchen, honey," Dad said. I was stunned, so helpless that I let him shut me in. I heard them tramping up the stairs. What could have happened to Mother that she needed an ambulance? Why didn't the doctor want me to see her? I opened the door to look, but all I saw was the bulky bodies of the men who were carrying her out the front door. I panicked. "Maa!" I bawled. I had never felt such misery. Something horrible had happened to my mother.

When I calmed down, the emptiness of the house got to me. All the mechanical creaks and hums had taken over. I needed to do something physical, so I began making coffee in the electric drip pot, putting in an extra scoop the way my father liked it. I opened a can of clam chowder, his favorite soup, and rummaged through the refrigerator for leftovers to make a meal for him. I didn't find much. Mother had been serving no-work things like cottage cheese and canned fruit or tuna fish for supper lately. I had figured she was dieting and didn't complain. Melted cheese sandwiches for lunch and dinner every day would satisfy my appetite anyway. Mother was the one who enjoyed food. She liked to fuss over elegant meals with candlelight and wine sauces—or she had until a few months ago, or was it a year? How long? She had changed. All the tiredness. The bizarre business with the needlepoint. She had lost her liveliness right under my eyes and I hadn't even noticed. Whatever was wrong with her hadn't been sudden at all.

Jennifer called to find out why I'd left her house without saying good-bye. I couldn't talk to her. "But we're going to Vermont tomorrow," she said.

"Have a good time," I said and hung up on her.

My father got back long past midnight. I had fallen asleep on the couch. "How is she?" I asked.

"Okay. They'll take care of her."

"But what does she have?"

"She's just down, that's all, a little depressed."

"Depressed? She never told me. I guess I should have seen it."

"Not you, honey, me. We see what we want to see." His thin face, which never showed his feelings, looked worried now.

I thought about it, but I didn't believe he was to blame. He was steady. He was kind. He always came home to us, and we were all he cared about besides flying, so far as I knew. It was me. I was the one who had changed. "My daughter's my best friend," Mother always told people and hugged me as if nothing could be nicer. Then I'd gone and found another best friend. Selfish, I thought. I am a rotten, selfish person.

My father kept stirring his soup. "You don't have to eat it, Daddy," I said, realizing he'd only told me to make him supper to give me something to do. He was convinced doing something physical made a person feel better. It was his suggestion that Mother take those exercise classes—Yoga, aerobics, slimnastics. He'd wanted her to run with him too, but she couldn't keep up, and though she learned tennis, she never got past the beginner stage. I was the one with whom he ran now, or swam or played tennis when he was home. Mother had been left out of that too.

He sighed. "I'll have the coffee anyway. Thanks, Kelly." I hugged him and cried and was glad to have him there with me.

* * *

The next morning when I woke up, Dad had already made arrangements for me to stay with my grandparents. Never mind that there was still a week of the school year to go. He was going to fly me down to Florida at dawn on Monday morning. I was to use Sunday to get packed while he did all the necessary things to close up the house, like leaving a note for the mailman and calling the police and the newspaper boy, who was now to cut our lawn. I was upset, especially when I couldn't even get hold of Jennifer to tell her what had happened. It took me a while to remember that she had gone to Vermont.

"You could have discussed my going to Florida with me first, Dad," I said. "I'm not such a baby that I couldn't stay in the house alone. Or I could move in with Jennifer. Her mother wouldn't mind."

He shook his head. "Don't give me a hard time, honey. I've got your mother and my job to worry about. I want you where I'm sure you're safe."

"But who's going to visit Mother in the hospital?"

"I will."

"When you're here," I said. "And suppose she's sick for weeks or months. What then?"

"Listen," he said. "I've got to be in Madrid this week. My bosses are in the middle of high-level negotiations with millions of dollars at stake. I can't afford to leave them in the lurch. They pay me too well to be there when they need me and I like my job, but I'll take off as much time as I can."

"That's what I thought," I said. "Then who's there for Mother when you're not?"

"Her doctor, Kelly, and I'll call Bea Mayer later in the week. Don't worry."

"At least let me see her before I leave."

"No."

"Why not?"

"Doctor's orders."

"How come? *Why* can't I see her?" My fear was making my voice shrill, and I could see the shutters closing over Dad's face. "Please!" I begged.

"Don't start acting like a baby on me," he warned.

"But what's happened to Mother? Why did she have to go to the hospital all of a sudden? She wasn't so sick. She was just tired all the time and feeling blue because—"

"Because of what?" he asked sharply. "Did she tell you anything?"

"Not really." I swallowed my guilt. I couldn't admit it was my fault. Not then.

"Cheer up," he said. "Maybe this will work out better for you than you think." He hugged me as if he understood my feelings a little after all. His strong fingers gripped my shoulder as he added, "Your grandmother is quite a lady, and you've never had a chance to get to know her." He smiled, coaxing me. His smile made his face go homely with too much nose and chin.

I loved him, but right then I wished he wasn't so hard to budge once he'd decided something.

"Look at all the swimming you can get in down there," he said. "It's not going to be so bad."

"I don't feel like swimming," I said. "Can you at least tell me when I can come home?"

"As soon as your mother's ready. As soon as the doctor advises it."

"It's not fair," I said bitterly and meant he wasn't fair. He heard it that way too. He withdrew into that cold silence that clamped down against us when he thought we were being unreasonable. His silence punished us worse than words. I saw the grim line of his mouth and obeyed when he told me to start packing.

He was my father. He should know what was best, but a piece had been torn from my life and I hurt. Why couldn't I have been allowed to say good-bye to her? Just the sight of Mother, even in a hospital bed, would have reassured me. As it was, the only way I could control my runaway fears was not to let myself think about her at all.

Chapter 3

We were in the taxi on the way from the airport to my grandparents' house, which is near Palm Beach. The air was hotter and more humid than I remembered from my visit six years ago, but that had been winter and now it was the middle of June. The houses we passed once we got off the highway were pink-and-white confections, mostly stucco with tile roofs. The palm fronds rattling in the wind and the feathery look of the Australian pines added to the foreignness of the landscape. "Bougainvillea," I said, recognizing a hedge full of clustered red flowerets whose name Mother and I had practiced pronouncing six years ago. My father sat silently beside me. Who knew when I'd have a chance to talk to him again.

"How am I going to find out how Mother's doing?" I asked. "Can I call her every night?"

"No. No phone calls at all yet. But don't worry. I'll let you know how she is, or your grandmother will. She can call the hospital."

"Mother will want to hear from me, Dad. There's nobody closer to her than me."

"Kelly, she is my wife. I love your mother too."

I was reassured to hear him say it even if I'd annoyed him. Dad hides his feelings so well, I sometimes doubt that he has any. He's basically a sealed-off sort of person.

The taxi stopped in front of the archway in the long, hedge-backed iron fence around my grandparents' property. I could see that the grounds had been neglected. The bushes had grown so monstrous that they took up too much space and seemed to be crowding in on us as we carried our suitcases to the front door. The tan stucco face of the flat-roofed house was streaked and patchy. I followed my father inside reluctantly, more than ever feeling as if I'd come to a foreign country.

The woman in maid's uniform who had opened the door for us went to fetch Grandmother while Dad and I waited in the anteroom. I looked up at the nymphs representing the four seasons painted on the high ceiling. Inside, the house was no less impressive than it had been to me when I was eight. Wood-paneled doors opened into the living room and dining room and Grandma's sitting room and Grandpa's library. Below the stairs, I knew, was an opening that led through a dark hallway to the huge kitchen. Everything inside looked the same as it had, even the bronze horseman, which I could see on the ornate wood-and-marble fireplace in the living room. My grandmother looked the same too, when she arrived. She's tall and thin like my father, with a hawk nose in a narrow face. Mother said a coronet should crown Grandmother's white hair, which she wears drawn back in a French knot. Once I'd asked Mother directly what was wrong with my grandparents. All she said was, "They're people who like to keep to their routines. We're just not part of their precious routines, I'm afraid." She wouldn't say more even when I questioned her. "They're your only grandparents, Kelly," was all she said. But I'd heard her say to my father, "She couldn't care less whether she sees us or not. How can she be so indifferent when you're her only son?" I thought it was an awful thing to say, a hurting thing, but my father had answered her casually.

"Well, we'll connect with them one of these days. It's bad timing, that's all." He wouldn't argue with Mother about his family. He didn't like to argue. It was Mother and I who lost our tempers regularly and fought it out and kissed and made up. Dad would simply be silent until his anger went away.

Grandmother turned to me after greeting my father and said, "What a pleasant surprise. You've grown up beautifully." She offered her cheek, which I kissed. I wondered if the surprise was that I'd grown up well or just in having me appear on her doorstep.

"Hello, Grandmother. It's nice to see you," I said dutifully, and let my hand be held in thin, papery fingers while she studied me.

"I hope this isn't going to be too much for you, Mother," Dad said. "I know you've got your hands full as is."

"Don't worry, Harvey. I have Corallee to help me with your father. The only difficulty is there's not much here in the summer to amuse a young girl. The clubhouse is closed for the season, you know. Everyone goes north except us."

"Kelly's very good at amusing herself. She's a reader and a swimmer," he said.

"Like her father," Grandmother answered him with a smile. "You were such a self-sufficient child, Harvey. Well, I'm sure we'll manage. And after all, it can't be helped, can it?"

She inquired about our trip and then led us through the living room to the patio in the garden where breakfast waited. Polite murmurs about toast and jam got me through breakfast while my father and grandmother talked, not about my mother, and not about the ghastly old man sitting in the chair across the table from me, staring at me with a stony look of horror, but about the weather and old friends with unfamiliar names. I jumped when the old man barked suddenly. He tried to rise from his chair. Grandmother leaned over and patted his arm comfortingly.

"Now, now, Charles. It's all right. We're just having breakfast with your son and his child. There, dear, there, sit down and have some muffin."

She held a piece of buttered muffin to the old man's lips. His tongue shot out like a lizard's and took the muffin. Then he chewed it as if it needed chewing. Now I understood. He hadn't been staring at me particularly. He wasn't focusing on anything here and now. My grandfather was senile. It was horrible, horrible and I was stuck here where nobody wanted me until my mother got well enough for me to return home. My throat was so dry I couldn't eat the rest of my toast or drink my café au lait.

When Dad said good-bye to me at the front door, I wanted to cry for a reprieve, but I knew it wouldn't do me any good. "Be brave," he'd say. The time he'd most approved of me was when I didn't cry while the doctor stitched me up because I'd fallen on a piece of glass while we were running.

"When will you be back from Madrid?" I asked him.

"In a few days."

"And will you write me or call as soon as you know something about Mother? You *will* call her doctor to find out how she is?"

"Every day, and I'll let you know as soon as anything changes. Listen, it's going to be all right."

He kissed me and touched his lips to Grandmother's cheek. The door closed behind him. I was alone with my grandmother. I looked at her, waiting to see what she would do. She gave me a tentative smile and said, "It's too bad this had to happen during our hibernating season. I dare say there isn't a soul under sixty within miles of us. Your grandfather and I used to travel during the summers. Now, of course, we just wait the heat out. One doesn't need to do much about time as one gets older. It just passes . . . Well," she said and looked at me as if she didn't know what came next either. "We'll just have to make the best of it. Would you like to see the library?"

The heels of Grandmother's sensible shoes clicked on the parquet floor as she left the blue-and-gold Chinese carpet in the entry hall. My gum-soled sandals didn't make a sound as I followed her through the paneled doors into Grandfather's library. He had been a college president once. Books lined the walls from floor to ceiling except between the windows where there were framed certificates and pictures of solemn men, a dagger with a jeweled hilt, a painting of the Taj Mahal with a museum light over it, a map of the ancient world. The big, leather-topped desk held a lamp and a jade paperweight. There were two matching leather armchairs on either side of a table below the front window. It was a solemn-looking room.

"I don't suppose the classics are your favorite reading material," Grandmother said. "Young people don't read them anymore, but you might try. There's a complete set of Dickens here and Thackeray. Shakespeare, of course. Most of your grandfather's books are scholarly tomes. He was a classics professor originally, you know."

"No," I said. "I didn't know. I'm sorry that he . . . It must be very hard for you . . ." I didn't know if I should say the word senile out loud.

"No," Grandmother said. "It's not hard for me at all. I love your grandfather. I stand by him now as he would have stood by me if our situations were reversed, that's all."

"That's beautiful," I said. I looked at her with admiration, understanding for the first time what my father had meant when he said she was quite a lady. Then to my own surprise, I burst out, "I don't understand what's happened to my mother. I don't know what I should do."

"There, there," Grandmother said in alarm. She touched my arm but withdrew her hand quickly. "You mustn't get upset. Your mother's being cared for. There's not a thing you can do except take care of yourself."

"But why did she get sick? What's wrong with her? Dad says she's depressed, but everybody gets depressed and they don't end up in a hospital." I wanted comfort, I guess, or maybe to hear that it wasn't really my fault, but Grandmother only looked anxious. I hurried on. "She's almost finished with a fine arts degree. She could go back and get that and then she'd have something to do and wouldn't feel like sleeping so much. Couldn't it be just that she's bored? I mean—"

"Dear child," Grandmother said, "there's no sense our discussing these things. What has happened has happened, and you must learn to cope."

"But I love my mother."

"Your mother needs professional help and is getting it. Now you must control yourself. We'll talk of something else." Grandmother stopped and seemed to reflect. Her mouth puckered as if she'd tasted something sour. "Perhaps you should go for a swim now before the beach gets too hot. The afternoon sun is much too strong. You must take care not to get burned."

I swallowed hard on my anger. "All right," I said. "I'll unpack and go to the beach."

Her relief was plain. "We have lunch at noon," she said. "Do please be on time. Your grandfather gets upset when anything interferes with his schedule." She told me how to find my room and left.

It was only nine o'clock. She'd disposed of me for the next three hours. Not that I minded getting away from her, but I needed desperately to talk to someone. I picked up the jade paperweight, which was in the form of a dragon. Now I saw it wasn't a paperweight at all, but a chop with my grandfather's name and a design, his personal seal probably. He had been an important man. He had won honors, been written up in the *Times* for talks he gave. And Grandmother had been prominent too. She'd had her picture in the newspapers often for charity things, for boards and balls and openings of hospital wings, and she had been beautiful, and she was my father's mother, my grandmother. I recalled all that and also, from the visit when I was eight, the sound of her voice saying to me, "Now be careful handling that, dear; it could not be replaced if you broke it . . . so fragile, silk . . . old paper tears easily . . . be careful . . . better not to touch." I had tiptoed around this house with my hands in my jeans' pockets looking with awe at all the lovely things my grandparents owned.

"Think you'd like to live in a museum, baby?" Mother had whispered to me when we were examining the porcelain figurines in the dining room.

"Not me," I'd said. "But look at the pretty blue glass bowl, Mother. Don't you just love it!"

At home everything was for touching, velvety coverings for the upholstered furniture instead of hard-surfaced silk, cushions to throw on the floor and lie against to read, old things that weren't quite antiques, on which another scratch wouldn't be noticed. My grandparents' house had impressed me nevertheless, and I had loved having the beach right beyond the garden wall. I remembered how Mother and I joined Grandmother for lunch at the clubhouse after she finished her morning chores, the board meeting she had to attend, the correspondence she had to deal with. Grandmother had been such a busy lady.

"How was the beach today?" she would ask, and Mother would chatter brightly to entertain her, about the man with the fringed sun hat and the Pekinese in his lap under the shade of an umbrella. Or she would weave a whole tale about the fisherman who caught a pailful while the surf casters on either side of him watched enviously. Mother had worked hard trying to entertain Grandmother. Now I realized what a hopeless task it had been.

I unpacked my suitcase slowly. The old-fashioned wardrobe on one wall of the room I'd been assigned still had plenty of drawer and closet space when I finished. This guest room had a window facing the beach; so I could look at the ocean and maybe even hear the waves beating time against the shore if they ever rose above the flat calm they showed today. I pulled the one comfortable-looking chair around so that I could sit and read and look out the window. No matter how bad things got, I'd have the ocean at least. The backboard of the high bed was carved, like the decorative borders around the wardrobe and dresser, with cornucopias of fruit. The rug was faded and threadbare in spots. I liked the room, though if it were really mine, I'd take down the flower paintings and put up Gauguin prints or the bright, splashy paintings Mother did. Mother. How was she this morning? Was she lying in a hospital bed wondering why I wasn't there? She'd want, at least, to hear my voice. I knew that, and I very much needed to hear hers.

I had my own bathroom off the bedroom—white-tiled floor and outsized white plumbing fixtures, with a bathtub with claw feet and wonderful lion's head faucets in the tub and sink. Posh! I looked at myself in the bathroom mirror, at my pale, pale skin which I hate and my narrow eyes like my father's, with his high-arched eyebrows. Mother's eyes are so much more beautiful. I wished for the millionth time I had her tip-tilted nose instead of my plain straight one. "You have such gorgeous cheek-bones," Mother always tried to console me. She said I was distinctive looking, beautiful instead of pretty. I'd much rather be pretty. But Gerry had liked what he saw when he looked at me. Had he been angry when he found out how old I was? Was he the kind of person to whom I could talk? Probably not. If only Jennifer were here. Mother, I thought, but it hurt so much to think about her that I clicked off my brain and hurried into my bikini. It was already past ten. I'd dawdled indoors long enough.

I ran downstairs expecting to slip out the kitchen way into the garden and to the beach, but the dark passage was blocked by a stumpy woman with an angry face and a tray full of medicine bottles, not the same woman who had opened the door for us.

"Where do you think you're going naked like that?"

"To the beach," I said.

"Well, you better get something to cover yourself with. You can't go walking through the house that way." The woman had a voice that pinched.

"Who are you?" I asked.

"I'm Corallee, your grandfather's nurse."

I wondered if I was obliged to obey her, but didn't have the patience to find out. I spun around and returned to my room for one of Dad's worn-at-the-neck dress shirts. It covered me to mid thigh. This time when I tried leaving, I made it through the overgrown garden, out the back gate and onto the beach.

Chapter 4

The beach was the same flat, dun-colored strip of sand I remembered. No dunes to make it interesting, but the water went from an incredible aqua to a sapphire blue a hundred feet off shore. The sea was so calm that I could hear the sudden flurry of bait fish leaping from the shallows. A lone gull skimmed the water. Otherwise nothing. Just blank, hot sand, salt air and me. I squeaked across the hard-surfaced sand in my flip-flops, dropped shirt and thongs a few feet from the water's edge and waded in expecting the shock of cold water, which didn't come. The water was lukewarm, so clear that as I swam I could see down to the bare bottom sand unmarked by rock or seaweed. I headed straight out, knowing I shouldn't, but feeling a need to do something reckless. The regular rhythm of my crawl strokes soothed me as usual. I should have been born a fish, I thought, maybe a manta ray, or a porpoise.

"You swim like a seal," my mother said. She

admires in me what she can't do herself. She said, "I may not be much, but I can always be proud of the daughter I produced." I shrugged off that praise without thinking past it to what she was saying about herself. Did she really believe she wasn't much? Why should she feel that way? Didn't I tell her often enough how wonderful she was? Unless it was my father she needed to hear it from . . .

When I turned and looked back at the shore, the gulls were smaller than golf balls. Too much water stretched between me and the beach. I rested, then began swimming back diagonally. I was glad Mother wasn't sitting there waiting for me and worrying. My arms got heavy. Gradually my muscles began resisting. I was relieved to reach the crumbling mini cliff of sand that edged this area of beach. I scrambled up it and looked back to where I'd started. Now the question was which of the roofs poking above the walled and fenced gardens behind the beach belonged to my grandparents' house. Looking at the row of roofs, red tile or white marble chips, some flat, some peaked, it occurred to me that all I had to do was find my discarded shirt and thongs. I wasn't lost at all.

As I walked, I studied a congregation of sea gulls. They faced seaward and pretended to ignore me, but they kept moving to maintain the distance between us as I got closer. I was so absorbed in the gulls and the way a minority of black-crested ones stuck together in their midst, that I didn't see the man in the wheelchair. When I did notice him, I tried not to stare at the malformed legs his swim trunks exposed. From the waist up, he was a good-looking blond man with an open smile. The smile was for me.

"Hi," I said when I was a few feet from him.

"Boy, am I glad to see you!" he said in a hearty voice that rang with confidence.

"Huh? Why?" I stopped in front of his balloon-tired wheelchair, which even had a little beach umbrella attached to one corner.

"I got the idea you were planning to swim the Atlantic," he said.

"I'm sorry I scared you. I like to swim."

"Yes, I can see that. Well, good for you, but it's dangerous to go so far out alone."

"Yes," I said. "You're right."

He stuck his square, freckled hand out. "I'm Evan Stone."

I grasped his hand and we shook briskly. "I'm Kelly Allgood," I said.

"Oh, the Allgoods' granddaughter. Great! We're next-door neighbors."

Grandmother had said there was nobody under sixty around. Didn't Evan count? "Do you swim?" I asked without thinking.

"Wish I could," he said.

"Oh, I'm sorry." My tactlessness embarrassed me. I had no experience at all with handicapped people.

"Hey, no problem," he said. "I'm used to being confined to my beach buggy. How do you like it? Isn't it nifty? My parents had it specially made for me when I was a kid so I could enjoy the beach."

"It's quite a vehicle," I said. I'd been out of the water only a few minutes and already I was oven dried. I stood storklike, cooling the sole of first one cooked foot and then the other against my calves.

"Hot?" he asked. "That's why this beach is so empty in the summer. Also it's nearly noon."

"Twelve o'clock?" I said. "That's when I'm supposed to be back for lunch."

"You better run. Tell your grandmother I'm going to stop by and say hello. I'm here to close my parents' house."

"I'll tell her. Nice meeting you." I waved as I dashed off, detouring to cool my feet in the ocean before scooping up my belongings at a run.

Once past the hedge of sea grape, hibiscus and palm, I saw my grandparents already seated at a glass table set for lunch.

"There you are." Grandmother didn't sound pleased.

"I'm not late, am I?" I gasped. "I had such a good swim I nearly forgot to come in."

"That's not too reassuring," Grandmother said in the same cool tone. "It's dangerous enough to swim alone here without your being reckless besides."

"I'm sorry I worried you, Grandmother."

"You do realize that you're my responsibility now?" she said. "I think you had better promise you won't swim beyond where you can touch bottom. Suppose you got a cramp? Or you could get caught in a riptide. It's happened to enough people hereabouts."

"I promise I'll be careful."

"Well, sit down. Your soup is waiting for you."

I took the chair between my grandparents, who sat facing each other, and draped my shirt over the back of it.

"In the future," Grandmother said, "do try to leave time enough to change into something civilized before you come to eat." Her smile didn't take the sting out of her rebuke.

I wondered how many weeks of Grandmother I was sentenced to, but having been taught to respect my elders, I lowered my eyes meekly and set to eating.

"While I am at it," Grandmother said more lightly, "perhaps I can ask another indulgence. Would you mind if I called you Kate?"

"Kate? Why?" I was startled. "What's wrong with my real name?"

"Your real name should have been Kate or Katherine. That was my mother's name. Your mother chose to take the first initial and turn it into Kelly, which is hoydenish. Kate suits you better."

Hoydenish I guessed must be something bad. "I prefer to keep the name my mother gave me," I said. I liked my name. A Kelly was bold; she would risk new things. The name had excitement and laughter in it, and if my grandmother didn't like it, well, that was her problem.

Grandmother sighed as if I were being difficult. Just then the woman who had accosted me in the hall that morning appeared. She ignored both Grandmother and me, tied an oversized linen napkin like a bib around my grandfather's neck, and began spooning soup into him. She was a teapot-shaped woman with thin limbs and a disagreeable expression.

"Have you met Corallee yet?" Grandmother asked me.

"We haven't been introduced," I said.

"Well then—" Grandmother put down her buttered roll and made formal introductions. Corallee acknowledged them with a grunt over one shoulder.

"Can't he feed himself?" I asked. It was disgusting to see a grown man treated like a baby.

"Not soup. He spills it," Grandmother said matter-of-factly.

"He can do a lot of things your grandma won't let him do just because he does them messy," Corallee said.

"Corallee has been so good for your grandfather," Grandmother overrode her smoothly. "Since she's come, he's relaxed considerably."

"But I ain't staying nights no matter what," Corallee said.

"We'll see," Grandmother said. "We must all do what has to be done."

"Not me. He ain't my kin. I got my own family to do for," Corallee said. Her voice was sharp as a splinter. It sounded as if this was an old battle between them and as if Corallee feared losing it.

"And I suppose you can find yourself a better job tomorrow?" Grandmother asked coolly.

Corallee clamped her lips shut and concentrated on feeding the old man his lunch. Besides the soup, there was a casserole of some kind of fish and a horn-shaped roll.

All the tension had taken my appetite away. I nibbled at my roll but left the soup uneaten.

"Aren't you hungry?" Grandmother asked.

"Not very."

"You must eat anyway. You're lean like your father and me. Thank heavens you don't take after her in that respect."

"Take after who? My mother? My mother's not fat," I said.

"It is better when one's bones show. Bones are handsome. Flesh is not," Grandmother said.

I laughed. She sounded so positive, and I knew she was wrong. No boy paid attention to me before I started putting flesh on strategic parts of my body. Flesh, in my experience, was much more attractive than bones.

"I hadn't intended humor," Grandmother said with a frown.

"What you said reminded me of something else," I offered.

"I hope," Grandmother said, "that it won't be too difficult for you to fit into our daily routines. You will have to, you know. We are too old to change."

"I won't be late again," I promised.

"That isn't to what I was referring. I gather your grandfather's condition is upsetting to your digestion." She put a slender hand, palm out. "Don't deny it. You have an expressive face. Well, my dear, your grandfather and I have been companions the greater part of our lives, and that companionship will remain until the end, however difficult life becomes for us."

"Of course," I said. She might be a tyrant, but she had read me very well. I would have said that I admired her loyalty to her husband, but I hadn't forgiven her for trying to change my name or for her lack of sympathy for my mother, so I picked up my spoon again and said only, "This soup is delicious. I never had cold soup before."

"You've never eaten vichyssoise? How odd."

"What's odd about it?"

"I suppose you're right. Your mother wouldn't be familiar with it. In this climate we have a cold soup for lunch most days."

"She's gonna burn tonight," Corallee said over her shoulder.

I was so angry at my grandmother that for a second I thought Corallee was talking about Hell, that she was some kind of religious fanatic. She looked as if she could be. Then I realized she was staring at my shoulders. Sure enough, my arms and shoulders were a fiery red.

"Corallee's right," Grandmother said. "You did get too much sun." She sounded genuinely concerned. "We had better put some healing ointment on you."

"I'm all right," I said. "Just going to peel, that's all."

The casserole was tasty. I wondered if they ate this elegantly every day and if Corallee or the maid who had opened the door for us was responsible for the cooking.

"I think there's something in the guest room medicine cabinet that will help. It's been there a while, but it should still be effective," Grandmother said.

"Bath with baking soda, that's the ticket," Corallee said. "Take the heat right out."

"Grandmother, I forgot to tell you," I said to change the subject. "I met a neighbor of yours on the beach this morning. Evan Stone. He said he'd stop by soon."

"The crippled fellow? He's down here? His parents both passed away last winter. I wonder what he's doing here in the hot season," Grandmother said.

Crippled fellow, I thought, indignant on Evan's behalf. "He seems very nice," I said.

"Oh, yes, he's a charmer. Works for a prestigious law firm in New York. He had polio as a child. Terrible thing. But I understand he manages to travel all over the world by himself in his wheel-chairs. He has one for every occasion. His parents indulged him. I can remember seeing him at the club, poor fellow, watching your father do laps in the pool when they were boys. It made me count my blessings."

"He's as old as my *father?* I thought he was in his twenties," I said.

"Yes, he looks young," Grandmother agreed. "I hope he does stop by. I'm interested in knowing what he plans to do with his parents' house."

"Grandmother," I said, figuring her mood was about as good now as it was likely to get, "may I make a long-distance phone call home tonight?"

"It's much too soon," she said and sat back in her chair while Corallee cleared the table. I had a sudden surge of homesickness. My darling mother was lying alone in a hospital bed thinking that her daughter had forgotten her entirely.

"I'm sure," I said, "that my mother would feel better if she heard from me."

"I believe you heard me say no," Grandmother said.

Rage filled me. I gritted my teeth to keep from blurting out something I'd regret, stood up, and began picking up the dirty dishes to stack on the tray Corallee was using.

"Meals is part of my job," Corallee said to me. "I see to your grandfather and do meals and leave here at six sharp."

"Corallee is not a trained nurse; she's more of a homemaker," Grandmother said when the tray had disappeared into the house in Corallee's hands. "However, she's efficient and dependable, two qualities one doesn't often find in help nowadays."

"I don't know anything about help. My mother does her own work," I said.

"Indeed," Grandmother said and continued. "After lunch, I usually read aloud to your grandfather here in the garden. Then we take our naps and have our aperitifs around four. We eat at five to accommodate Corallee, an ungodly hour, but there it is. Now, can you find something to occupy you for the afternoon?"

It was dismissal time. Quickly I said, "I don't understand why I can't call my mother today. I wish you'd explain that to me."

She stared at me, handsome in her silent anger. If I hadn't been so angry myself, I would have been scared. "It is her doctor's orders that you are not to get in touch with your mother, not my whim as you seem to think. You must learn patience. Young people are always so impatient." She rose slowly. "I'm reading a travelogue to your grandfather on Yugoslavia where we once spent a few lovely weeks with friends in Dubrovnik. Would you care to listen?"

"No, thank you. I'll go up to my room," I said. It was useless to argue with her, but I didn't believe that any doctor would keep a patient from hearing from her own child. It had to be my grandmother who had decided to drive me away from my mother. How dare she look down on my mother! Who did my grandmother think she was anyway? Just having a lot of money didn't make her special. I had never hated anybody, but I was beginning to hate her.

Chapter 5

"Dear Mother," I wrote. "Here I am stuck under the royal thumb of the Queen Mother. You sure picked the right name for her. Well, I'll survive, I hope. What I really want to know is how you are . . ." I considered. I wanted to ask Mother if I was to blame for her getting sick. How to phrase such a naked question? I tried and couldn't get it right. Then I decided it didn't matter. My mother would never admit I'd failed her. I was her wonderful, perfect daughter. She wouldn't let go of that ideal.

"I want to come back home. I need to see you," I wrote. "I can't stand thinking of you being sick all alone. I don't understand what's wrong with you, but I know you want me with you no matter what anybody says."

I stared out at the brilliant striping of sand and dark blue sea and light blue sky, a tricolored flag framed by the window. What had happened was unbelievable. Mother in the hospital and me in my grandparents' house. It couldn't be my fault. I was fourteen years old. A girl isn't responsible for her mother. It was supposed to be the other way around. Besides, I hadn't done anything terrible. Spending my free time with Jennifer, that wasn't terrible. But if it would make Mother well, I'd give up Jennifer and boys—anything now.

"Mother," I wrote, "you must get well for my sake. I need you and I love you very much." I underlined *very* four times. Then I considered what else to tell her. The incident with Gerry that had sent me running home Saturday night seemed long past. Instead of panicking, I should have just told him firmly to quit it. He would have. He wouldn't have dared risk his reputation with his cousin. Instead of running home, I should have gone back inside and talked to Jennifer. I thought of all the things I could have said to Gerry, all the ways I should have acted. But he had been awful. I sighed. If only I could talk to someone!

My shoulders were burning. It hurt to lean back against the chair. I went to the bathroom medicine cabinet and found the sticky white ointment Grandmother had mentioned. Gingerly I patted it onto my shoulders while I tried to reason my way out of my confusion. Wrong to imagine Mother would want me to stop seeing Jennifer. Mother had always encouraged me to make friends. It had been due to Mother that Jennifer and I got together in the first place.

"You like drama so much," Mother had said to me last summer. "Why don't you take a class in improvisation the museum is offering? My friend Bea Mayer has a daughter who's going to take it. We could carpool. Bea's daughter is a couple of years older than you, but a very sweet, open girl. You might like her."

From the first session of the course, when Jennifer and I were to pretend to be stuck in an elevator together for our improvisation, we had gotten along well. We went to the film series at the museum together, Jennifer and Mother and I. Jennifer's mother didn't like old films, and besides, it was about then that she got a job as an office manager. For a while Jennifer and Mother and I spent lots of afternoons and evenings together. "Your mother is such fun to be with," Jennifer said, and she commented, "I think your mother enjoys our company more than her own friends'." Although as an afterthought, Jennifer did question whether Mother had any friends.

"My mother has lots of friends. Everybody likes her," I answered. It had been true when I was small. Now Bea was the only person Mother still heard from occasionally.

After Jennifer began seeing Mark, she became shy about including Mother in her confidences. She would talk to me about her sex life, but Mother was a married woman. "I know you tell your mother everything, Kelly," Jennifer would say to me, "but I'll never forgive you if you blab this."

"I don't blab your private business," I promised.

"No, I can trust you," Jennifer said. "That's why you're my friend." Sometimes Jennifer invited me along with Mark to what her mother considered a safe enough threesome. We'd go in Mark's father's car to a hockey game or skiing. Jennifer's mother was strict. Unless I was along, she wouldn't allow Jennifer to go very far away with Mark. Occasionally when the three of us were together, Jennifer would say, "You don't mind staying here alone a while, Kelly? We'll be right back." I'd watch the game, waiting patiently for them, or sit and read a book, knowing what they needed to be alone to do. I didn't mind. I was glad to be of use to my friend. Sometimes, Mother would ask if I wouldn't like to go shopping with her or to a movie. She didn't complain when I said no, but her voice would get wistful. I did leave her alone too much, but then if she'd wanted companionship, she could have found it.

I finished my letter to my mother with a description of Grandfather's condition and a sketch of Corallee and Evan. The letter was eight pages long. I addressed it to the hospital and was about to ask Grandmother to mail it for me when I reconsidered. Why not use the hours until "aperitif" time to explore this neighborhood? There had to be a post office within a couple of miles. I scribbled a quick note to Jennifer.

". . . I need your help. Please ask your mother to find out how my mother is doing and let me know as soon as you can. If you could get Bea to visit Mother in the hospital, I'd really appreciate it. I don't understand what's wrong with her, but they don't want me to contact her. Isn't that weird? I'm beginning to get suspicious that my grandmother is deliberately keeping me from Mother. I don't know what to think and I'm really desperate. Love, Kelly." I tucked the note into the flower-lined envelope that matched the border of the stationery Jennifer had given me for my birthday. Good thing I'd remembered to pack it.

It was after two when I slipped downstairs and out of the front door. Almost two hours until aperitif time. Cocktails was probably what that meant. Two new words in one day—hoydenish and aperitif. I'd better locate a dictionary fast. My skin felt tight and tender despite the ointment. I'd worn the lightest thing I owned, but even the touch of my loose cotton sunback's straps hurt. The empty street was shaded by trees with talkative birds hidden in the overhanging branches. The air was so moist and sweet it was like walking through a hothouse. Each home had some special ornament, I noticed. One had a magnificent gate, another a well-watered lawn with a fountain spewing water from dolphins' mouths. But I had the eerie feeling that I was walking through a peopleless landscape. No one even to ask directions from. The taxi had crossed a shopping street this morning, but I had no idea how far it was or if I was going toward it or not.

A sleek gray car purred toward me and turned into a driveway. A white-haired man with a mustache climbed the wide steps to the verandah of a Spanish mission-style house. He looked as distinguished as I remembered my grandfather looking six years ago. I felt a quick pity for my grandmother. It had to be terrible for her to see him with that horrified stare as if he couldn't believe what had happened to him, terrible for both of them.

A display of seashells in the picture window of a modern house close to the street caught my eye. A host of shell ladies could live in those shells, mostly murexes, big ones with spiny fringes and intricate curves. Or was it only on beaches that shell ladies lived?

"The Lady Barbara had such a beautiful voice," I could hear Mother saying in my head, "that her husband loved above all things to hear her singing. In fact, when he went off to war, he promised that if she kept on singing, he would be sure to return to her. Now Lady Barbara adored her husband. So daily she stood on the point of land from where she'd watched him sail away and sang into the wind. From morning until the last embers of the dying day faded from the sky, through storms and icy winds she sang until, as years passed, her voice grew hoarse.

"One day a ship came near shore, and a bearded, battle-scarred warrior called out to ask the lady who she was and why she sang. She croaked back her answer as well as she could. The warrior raised a bow, and before she could run, he shot an arrow through her heart.

"'Some witch has taken the form of my wife and pretends to be her, but I know the lovely voice of the Lady Barbara and am not deceived,' the warrior, her husband, said. His ship sailed into port while she lay bleeding, but before her spirit left the earth, the king of the sea rescued her and placed her in a lovely shell. There she continues to sing forever for the husband she loved so faithfully."

When I asked Mother once if she minded that Dad was gone so much of the time, she said, "I don't like it, but I have to live with it because he loves his job, Kelly. He'd be miserable if he couldn't fly."

Odd that Mother's fairy tales were sad. She wasn't sad about real things. She said life was already too full of negatives and that a person ought to look for the sunshine and keep smiling. Now I wondered, were the shell lady stories just fairy tales or were they true? Was my mother a shell lady, one of them, all of them? She had seemed to me to be a happy person. She got such pleasure from ordinary things. She'd get excited about hanging crisp new curtains at the kitchen window, or she'd go giddy in an antique shop over an old medicine bottle that was the perfect shade of blue. She was always learning the words to new songs and singing. She was a happy person. Unless the sadness was so well hidden that I'd never found it.

I had walked half a mile at least and was still in a tree-shaded residential area of big homes, nothing commercial, not even any of the high-rise condominiums that we'd passed yesterday. I could ask Grandmother to mail the letters or wait for a mailman tomorrow and ask him. Even if Grandmother was really an ogre, she wouldn't stop me from writing a letter to my mother. Or would she?

A truck with the sign Atlas Gardeners painted on it passed me and pulled into a driveway. The driver was a black man with a grizzled beard and baggy pants. His face looked peaceful. He was unloading a lawnmower down the ramp behind his pickup when I asked him, "Could you tell me where there's a post office near here?"

He stopped working and considered. "Seems there's one hereabouts but I can't recall where. You got to mail something?"

"Yes," I said.

"Well, best you get someone to drive you. It's gonna be too far to walk in this heat."

"I don't think my grandparents drive," I said.

"Mailman probably come by and help you out," he said and bent over to fill the mower from a red can of gasoline.

"Excuse me," I said in desperation. "Could you possibly help me? Do you pass a post office anywhere? I'd be glad to pay you to mail these letters for me."

"Well . . . . " He hesitated. "There is a post office right by my house. I maybe could stop there for you."

I dug my wallet out of my pocket, thanking him while I handed the letters and enough money to cover postage and what I hoped would be a tip.

"That's all right," he said handing me back most of the money. "You don't have to pay me nothing extra."

I didn't know if the tip was too small or if he really was just glad to be of service to a stranger, but I thanked him awkwardly a few more times. He put the letters on the dashboard of the his truck. I wondered if they were going to get mailed or tossed out, but smiled at him as he nodded and walked off pushing the noisy mower. Should I have left the letters with him or would I have been better off waylaying the mailman? I wondered as I walked home. Stop worrying, I told myself. He said he'd do it. Was it because he was black that I didn't trust him? I mulled that over and finally excused myself. No, not because he was black but because he was a stranger.

"Don't take favors from a stranger," Mother had taught me. "You never know if they're really nice or not until it's too late." And it wasn't just the kind of warning a mother gives a little girl to keep her out of a pervert's hands, it was Mother's way. I could remember being lost in Boston with her and having a man on the street ask if there was anything wrong. "No," Mother had said and walked away as fast as she could with me dragging behind her. She waited until we came to a store to ask for directions. In my experience most people are nice, but Mother doesn't seem to trust people, though why she shouldn't, I don't know. Maybe I knew my mother less well than I had thought. If she'd been hiding behind a smile all these years, then what was she really like? It disturbed me to think the person I was closest to in the whole world was someone I didn't know well at all.

Chapter 6

"They're out in the garden, and your grandma's plenty mad at you," Corallee said as she passed me with a tray of hors d'oeuvres in her hands. "You're lucky she's got company. You won't get it till he leaves."

"Thanks a bunch, Corallee," I said. "You sure know how to make a girl feel good."

My sarcasm didn't faze her. She marched off, hor d'oeuvres raised on high. If Corallee had a heart, I suspected it was made of stainless steel. I stepped through the French doors and closed them behind me, leaving the air-conditioned house reluctantly. My grandparents, who seemed immune to the humid heat of a Florida summer, were sitting on the tiled patio in garden chairs. Evan was there too in his wheelchair, wearing a dressy-looking light cotton jacket, shirt and shorts. His warm greeting lifted my spirits.

"There she is, the little mermaid herself!" he said. "How're you doing, Kelly?"

"We've been waiting for you, young lady," Grandmother said with a half-inch smile that showed her annoyance.

"I took a walk and got a little lost. The streets around here all look so much alike," I said and added, "I'm sorry." But I resented having to make so many apologies there at my grandparents' house when normally I don't do things that need apologies.

"Wow," Evan said. "That's some sunburn you've got. Does it hurt?"

"Not yet. Much. I'll just look like a mess when I peel."

Evan laughed. "You'd be the prettiest sight on the beach, peeling or not. Listen, I have a lotion that will fix you up. I'll go get it."

"That's not necessary," Grandmother said. "We have an adequate supply of unguents in the house. Perhaps you should give yourself a first-aid treatment now."

I could tell Grandmother had spoken to me because she was looking right at me, but as usual, she'd avoided using my name. If I wasn't going to be Kate, I was going to remain nameless apparently.

"I'll be back in a minute. Don't go 'way, Evan," I said and raced upstairs to take care of my shoulders. I hurried so that I wouldn't miss much of Evan's company.

Back downstairs again, I sat in the chair next to my grandfather and sipped thirstily at the ginger ale with lemon peel waiting for me.

"Who are you?" Grandfather asked abruptly.

I jumped. I hadn't known he could talk. "I'm Kelly, your granddaughter," I said.

"Who are you?" he asked again as if I hadn't answered him.

"Charles, it's all right," Grandmother said. "It's Harvey's daughter come to visit us. Isn't that nice?"

He looked at Grandmother and seemed to forget me. I felt so sorry for him. Just above his shoulder, like a corsage, hung a spray of red frangipani that overreached the low hedge of variegated red, yellow and green leaves bordering the patio. The flowers made a sad contrast to his ravaged face. I breathed in the honey-sweet perfume of the garden and told myself that at least he had a beautiful home to live in and someone who loved him to take care of him. He had my mother beat by a mile.

"It's too elaborate an establishment to keep up for myself," Evan was saying, "and I'd rather sell it than see the place deteriorate."

"But all those lovely things your parents had! Surely you'll preserve their treasures?"

"Unfortunately my apartment in New York is small. Of course, I'll hang on to a few things for their sentimental value. A friend of mine is coming down to help me sort out what's to be kept and what's to be sold or given away. I'm sure some of Mother's ivory belongs in a museum."

"Such a pity, such a terrible pity that the most precious belongings of one's life are discarded so quickly."

"As long as they've been enjoyed while one's alive," Evan said, "that's the point, isn't it?"

"Beautiful objects endure where people do not. Things should be kept in the family. They're all we have of immortality," Grandmother said firmly. When Evan didn't agree, her eyebrows rose and she said, "You won't get rid of your father's snuffbox collection surely?"

"It's packed for sale. I have to confess Dad's snuffbox collection always seemed the height of the ridiculous to me."

"But they were your father's and he loved them."

"He loved collecting them," Evan said. "He enjoyed the chase. I'm sure he wouldn't resent my disposing of his trophies. Dad was never one to inflict his interests on anyone else."

"I should think you would want to keep them if only to remember him by."

"But I already have so much to remember my father by," Evan said. "Thirty-five years of loving memories."

"Yes, I suppose." Grandmother looked uncertainly at her husband. "Yes," she said, and after a while, she admitted, "You're quite right, Evan."

"So," Evan turned to me. "I understand your mother's ill, Kelly. Have you heard how she's doing?"

"No," I said, and would have explained why not if Grandmother hadn't interrupted.

"That reminds me, dear," she said. "Your father called. He wanted to speak with you, but you were out. He said to tell you your mother's condition is unchanged."

"Won't he call back so I can talk to him myself?" I couldn't believe this was all the message I was going to get.

"I'm sure he'll call again in a few days. Perhaps he'll be able to catch you in then."

She was implying that it was my own fault I'd missed his call. I was speechless. Not only did I not like my grandmother, but she obviously didn't like me either.

"Mrs. Allgood," Evan said in his compelling voice, "do you remember the time your son saved my life?"

"Vaguely," Grandmother said. "I remember hearing about it, not from Harvey. Harvey was never one to boast."

"I didn't know you even knew my father." I turned to Evan with surprise.

"Well, we weren't friends, if that's what you mean by know," Evan said. "But I admired your dad."

"Tell me what happened," I asked, eager to hear about my father's past.

"Well," Evan began, "my mother used to take me to the club every day. I'd sit in the shade and watch Harvey swimming and diving. I never saw anyone concentrate so hard on what he did as your father, and of course, he made it look easy. I figured I could swim too if I tried. So one day when my mother was occupied elsewhere and the pool was empty, I wiggled out of my wheelchair and plopped in—at the deep end, mind you. I was nothing if not self-confident. My arm muscles were strong and I expected it would be a cinch to imitate Harvey. Well, needless to say, I sank straight to the bottom, and there I would have stayed if Harvey hadn't noticed my empty wheelchair and jumped in after me."

"That's wonderful," I said. "I mean, that my father saved your life."

"Yes, I thought so too." Evan laughed. "But I was so humiliated at almost making a corpse of myself that I never properly thanked him."

"I'm sure you did and anyway, he wouldn't have wanted thanks," Grandmother said.

"No," Evan said. "I don't suppose my ingratitude affected him at all."

"I'm going to ask him about it next time I speak to him," I said.

"Do that. I'd be interested to know if he remembers," Evan said. "He'll probably say, 'That fool cripple, I should have let him drown.'"

"He wouldn't!" I said, shocked. "How could he think a thing like that about you?"

Grandmother clinked the ice cubes in her tall drink and said, "Evan's not serious, dear. . . . She's the image of her father, don't you think, Evan?"

"I may look like my father," I objected, "but inside I'm more like my mother."

"Let's hope you've inherited your father's constitution as well as his looks," Grandmother said. "He comes from strong stock."

"So does my mother."

"Does she?" Grandmother said as if she didn't think so. Then she asked Evan if he'd care to have another drink.

"No, thank you," he said. "I should be getting back to the house. I'm expecting my friend to call me from the airport. Kelly, if you have time, come over and visit us. We can always use a hand boxing and labeling things or even just an excuse to stop working."

"Thank you," I said. "I'd like that." I was still stiff with outrage at my grandmother's put-down of my mother.

Evan took my grandfather's hand and said, "Good-bye, Mr. Allgood." To my surprise, Grandfather half rose in his seat in response to the courtesy. He sat down again only when Evan said, "Don't bother getting up, sir. It's all right. Good seeing you." He patted Grandfather's hand and released it.

Grandmother looked pleased. She followed Evan as he wheeled himself through the house to the front door. I heard her telling him to come again soon. I was glad Evan had invited me over. Despite being disabled, Evan was a dynamic person, and I liked him a lot. Tomorrow, since I was too burned to go swimming again, I would visit him.

After Evan left, I was tempted to ask my grandmother outright why she despised my mother, but instead, I took myself up to my room. I was too angry with the Queen Mother to risk asking her anything tonight.

Chapter 7

At breakfast I tried again to move my grand-mother. "If I could call the hospital and speak to Mother or even to her doctor, I'd feel so much better," I said.

"Don't you believe what you're told?" Grand-mother asked, frowning at me as she tapped the top off the shell of her soft-boiled egg.

I put down my glass of orange juice. "A phone call's not so expensive," I said. "Anyway, I'd be glad to pay for it." I had ten dollars in my wallet to cover me in case my offer didn't embarrass her and she did relent, but she wasn't to be tricked.

"It's not the cost of a phone call that's in question. As I've already told you, your mother's doctor advises that she not be disturbed," Grandmother said.

"I'm her daughter. She loves me more than anybody. I *know* she'll feel better hearing from me." I did not believe the doctor's orders excuse.

"She was hearing from you every day, wasn't she,

and that didn't stop her from falling apart," Grandmother snapped.

"My mother didn't want to get sick," I said. My fingers clenched on the forkful of omelet. I knew I sounded shrill, but I couldn't help myself. I was sorry I'd let Grandmother cook that omelet for me, but she had seemed to want to be nice to me this morning. Her niceness hadn't lasted long.

"Your mother has a capacity for exaggeration," Grandmother said. "She's a highly emotional person. I'm sure she'll recover when she understands she's not gaining the attention she's seeking."

I shook with rage as I said, "What are you saying? That my mother *wants* to be sick? That's not true. She enjoys life more than anybody. People like her because she's so cheerful. She doesn't need to act sick to get attention." I stopped for breath. How dared she criticize my mother! But my temper didn't faze Grandmother one bit.

"From what your father tells me, your mother hasn't been enjoying life for quite a while. He indicates she's been withdrawing more and more in recent years. Of course, given her background, something like this was to be expected sooner or later."

Now we had come to it. "What's wrong with my mother's background?" I demanded. "Just because she's not rich . . . Having money doesn't make you a better person."

"Young lady, I don't like your tone. I don't like it at all. Hasn't your mother taught you any manners?"

"How can I have manners when you're insulting her?"

"Enough!" Grandmother commanded. She looked

as if she was about to order my head cut off, but I was too upset to care. I stood up and left my uneaten omelet to run upstairs to my room, nearly knocking over the maid who was dusting the picture frame at the head of the stairs. I couldn't stand another minute in Grandmother's company. Whatever she had against my mother didn't matter. She was my mother's enemy and that made her mine too.

When I'd calmed down, I put on a long-sleeved shirt over my halter top and picked up the broad-brimmed beach hat that Grandmother had lent me last night. She suggested I wear it outdoors until my sunburn healed. I didn't want to touch anything of hers, but my nose was too sore to endure more sun. What I aimed to do was run off.

Barefoot, I made no sound on the staircase and was at the front door before I hesitated. Then reluctantly, I called over my shoulder that I was leaving for the beach and would be back by noon. If Grandmother heard me, fine, if not, so be it.

It occurred to me that Evan might let me use his phone to make a long-distance call, but it was early and I didn't want to wake him up. Better to sweat out my emotions on a short run and then go see him. Even though the day smelled new and bird tracks were delicately pressed in the wet, cool sand, the air was already warm and heavy with moisture. Clouds blocked off the sun. The water near shore was that incredible gemstone aqua-marine and practically motionless in an early morning calm. I began to run, watching to see I didn't step on anything sharp, like a chunk of coral.

". . . given her background," Grandmother had said as if my mother's background was a disease.

Mother had told me about her family. I knew they were poor. They all lived in the same little country town in West Virginia and worked in garages or diners or the mill. Mother was the only one of her brothers and sisters who'd left home. She sent them Christmas cards although she rarely got any back, especially since her parents died. "When I left town," she'd explained to me, "it was like I rejected them and they held it against me. I took your father to visit once after we were married, but all they saw was how different my life was from theirs. I think they thought I was showing off. Well, I was in a way because I'd been the ugly duckling."

"But weren't any of your brothers or sisters glad to see you happily married?" I asked.

"I don't know, honey. I guess they figured that because my clothes were nicer than theirs and I talked better that I was putting on airs. They're a measuring kind of people. They don't like anyone who has more than they have."

"They don't sound very nice," I said.

"Oh, they're all right, I guess, just not much for writing letters. Anyway, I don't have good memories of my childhood to pull me back there. I hated my growing-up years. My Daddy could be nice sometimes, but my mother had a mean streak and she took it out on me."

If anything, it seemed to me my mother should have Grandmother's admiration for becoming such a lovely person despite her family.

On my way back, I saw Evan on the beach in his wheelchair with a crowd of squawking sea gulls hovering above and around him. I gasped. It looked as if the birds were attacking him while he sat helpless in his chair. As I sprinted across the hard sand to his rescue, the sea gulls flew up and away. Then I saw the plastic bag in his lap from which he was tossing up food to feed the gulls. I stopped short. One last bold gull swooped down to grab the piece of bread from Evan's extended fingers.

"Hi," Evan greeted me. "Have a good run?"

"You scared me. I thought they were attacking you."

He laughed. "We seem to make a practice of scaring each other. Yesterday it was your turn, today mine. Well, thanks for racing to my rescue."

"It's those mean-looking beaks," I said feeling foolish. "Plus I saw a movie on TV once and ever since I don't trust gulls up close."

"They're scavengers," he said, "but I suspect the worst I'm chancing is being shat on for my favors. How's it going, Kelly? Could you sleep with that sunburn?"

"I slept on my stomach. Nothing stops me from sleeping. . . . Evan, could I ask a big favor of you?"

"What can I do for you?"

"Let me make a long-distance call on your telephone."

"Be my guest. The phone's in the front room of the house. Just go straight through and to the left."

I hesitated. I didn't like to enter his house alone when I'd never been there before. "Did your friend come?" I asked.

He smiled wryly. "No. That's why I'm out here distracting myself by feeding the gulls. She called and said she has a patient in critical condition and can't leave him. She's a cardiologist."

"I'm sorry she disappointed you." I was a little

surprised that his friend was a woman, but then why shouldn't he have a female friend?

"No matter. So long as she gets here eventually. If I've learned anything from my life, it's patience. Want a guide to the telephone?"

"Please."

"Your grandmother still giving you a hard time?"

"Yes."

"She's a formidable lady, your grandmother, admirable in her way, but hard to live with, I bet."

'Very hard, especially for me."

He propelled his balloon-tired chair into a deeply shaded garden, overgrown with broad-leaved green bushes, huge spiky yucca plants and trees. The path circled an empty fish pond with a statue of a nymph pouring water from a pitcher in the center. At the foot of a ramp up the broad stone steps onto a terrace, Even let down the side of his chair and pulled himself over onto a smaller, sleeker wheelchair, the one he'd used at Grandmother's house. "Nifty?" he asked, showing me how easily it turned and cornered.

"Nifty," I said impressed that he was so well adjusted. I didn't think I'd ever get over feeling sorry for myself if I were confined to a wheelchair for my whole life. He led the way through rooms that were even more palatial than my grandparents'. The hallway was lined with cloth tapestries in which gowned and bewigged ladies minced through castle gardens and knights rode prancing horses with banners flying. Pillars like the columns in a Greek temple held up the ceiling in the center hall.

"It's so fancy," I said in awe.

"It is, isn't it?" Evan chuckled. "My parents did

not believe in the simple life. Can you see me fitting these furnishings into a small New York City apartment?"

"I wouldn't know," I said, glancing into the living room, which was full of gilded furniture and had creamy paneled walls and paintings with ornate gold frames. "I didn't know people really lived in places like this."

"Not too many people do. Wait until you see the phone. It's a gem." He led me to a table flanked by two matching gold-and-green chairs with tassels. The mirror I looked into was wreathed with gold leaves and berries. The narrow, dark-haired girl with the cherry red nose, silly looking beach hat and sloppy shirt looked like a clown in it. On the table was a telephone in white-and-gold enamel decorated with scenes of shepherdesses. "Like it?" he asked.

"I don't believe it," I said. "Does it work?"

"Would you believe it does that too?" Evan said. "Go ahead and make your call while I fix us something cool to drink. I'll be out on the terrace when you're done."

He was so tactful that he hadn't even asked me who I wanted to call. I got the telephone number of the hospital from information. Then I dialed and asked to speak to my mother. To speed things up, I warned the person who answered, "This is a long-distance call."

Patient information told me, "I'm sorry; there's no telephone in that room."

"Well, can you tell how my mother is?"

"Her condition is listed as fair."

"But then isn't there some way I can speak to her? Could she call me?"

"I can't answer that. Would you like me to connect you with someone in the psychiatric unit?"

"The psychiatric unit?" I asked, appalled.

I waited anxiously for the next voice, which turned out to be a nurse who gave me her name and asked what she could do for me. Again I was told I couldn't speak to my mother. This time the nurse added, "Don't worry; I'll tell her you called."

"Well, can she call me back, please?"

"Not yet, dear. She's under medication."

"But what's she taking medicine for? What's wrong with her? When will she get better? Can't someone answer me?"

"You'll have to speak to Dr. Bache. We're not allowed to divulge that information. Don't you worry though. We're taking good care of her."

Were they? I was now imagining my mother lying in a straitjacket, totally out of it without anyone who loved her nearby and surrounded by screaming maniacs. Something awful had happened to her. That was why they'd whisked her out of the house before I could see her and that was why they wouldn't let me speak to her now. Maybe I'd never speak to my mother again. In desperation I ran out to the terrace. "Evan! Do you know anything about depression?"

"Why?" he asked.

"My mother's in the hospital because she's supposed to be depressed, but they won't let me talk to her and I can't believe anything anyone's telling me anymore."

"Hey, take it easy," he said. "Sit down and have some lemonade and let's consider this thing."

I sat down, calmed somewhat by the strong timbre of his voice.

"So you were calling your mother?" he said. "I thought you might have a boyfriend you didn't want your grandmother to know about."

"Grandmother said I couldn't talk to my mother. I can't believe my mother wouldn't want to talk to me."

"Sure, but listen, Kelly, if she's severely depressed, they probably have her knocked out with antidepressants right now. Or maybe they're trying out different medications, and until they get the right formula, she won't be functioning normally. You understand? They may feel it would scare you to talk to your mother right now. Or she may be too out of it to respond to you yet. Your grandmother's an iron lady—the Grand Duchess was what I used to call her as a kid—but she's not a mean person. She wouldn't deliberately keep you from your mother."

"Oh, wouldn't she? She hates my mother. She talks as if my mother's a piece of dime-store junk." My lips twisted and my throat swelled and the tears poured out.

"Hey, now," he said patting my arm. "It can't be as bad as all that. Your mother will come out of it. People recover from depression all the time. Doctors know how to treat it now. They'll have her back on her feet in a few weeks or maybe a few months."

"How do you know?" I asked between sobs.

"I know because I've been there," he said. "I had my bout with depression after I graduated from law school and couldn't find anybody who'd hire me. It was tough and for a while I just gave up. I felt that nothing I did could change my life. I'd tried and nothing worked. Anyway I got help, and came out of it."

"My mother isn't just trying to get attention and giving in to herself the way Grandmother says."

"Of course not. Your grandmother's old school. She probably thinks mental illness is a failing of the will and shows a weak character. Right?"

"Depression is a mental illness?"

"It's a sickness. Sometimes it's caused by a chemical imbalance. Does that bother you, Kelly, to think of your mother as mentally ill?"

"Yes."

"Why? Your mother can't help being sick. It's like catching the flu. There's nothing to be ashamed of and it doesn't mean you're less of a person for getting it."

I looked at him. I admired him, and I loved and admired my mother. He was right. Suffering from depression didn't go with weak character. I took a deep breath and thanked him for talking to me so personally.

"Sure," he said. "Listen, instead of worrying, what you can do for your mother is show her plenty of love. Love and support, that's as powerful as any medicine."

I looked at him wide eyed. He'd gone too far. He'd as much as told me that I'd failed my mother. She had needed me and I hadn't stood by her. I'd been pulling away from her all year. Instead of showing her my love, I'd been impatient with her need for me. If I hadn't left her alone so much so I could run around with Jennifer, Mother might not be in that psychiatric unit.

"What's the matter?" he asked.

"Nothing."

"I must have said something. You look as if I hit you."

"No. I'm all right." Love and support—the words echoed in my head. Love and support—that was the least due to a mother as lovable as mine. "I think I'll run some more," I said.

"In this heat? You want to kill yourself?"

"No . . . I just feel like running."

"You know best," he said as if I puzzled him. "I'll save the lemonade for next time you stop by."

"Thanks for letting me make the phone call," I said.

I straggled back onto the beach. I didn't really feel like running, just like being alone. At the water's edge, I began to jog in case he was watching. A white sail was pasted on the dark blue horizon line between the sea and the lighter blue of the sky. Rumpled clouds in shades of gray and white were crammed together overhead. Low tide had left a dead fish that stank and lacy foam frills where the waves had touched. I watched for shells and tried not to think, but my mind ran with me.

She had given me clues and still I hadn't noticed. "I feel as if my skin's crawling so bad I want to rip it off," she had said, and what had I answered her?

"You better see a doctor, Mother."

"You used to tell me your dreams," she had complained. "You don't anymore. Why, Kelly?"

"My dreams aren't worth telling," I'd said when the truth was they were too embarrassing to share. My daydreams were full of boys being devastated by me, adoring boys to whom I granted all sorts of liberties with my body, and then, and then . . . getting excited lying in bed and touching myself. I couldn't tell my mother that. Even as close as we were, I hid my curiosity about sex. I wasn't the sweet little girl Mother had called her best friend anymore. My imagination didn't dwell on tragic shell ladies left to freeze on a rock by the sea until a handsome prince sailed by to rescue them.

"Tell me a happy story about a shell lady," I had asked her long ago.

"There are no happy stories about shell ladies. They wouldn't be shell ladies if they were happy. They're only allowed to live because their lives were so terribly sad."

"You're not sad, are you, Mother?" I had asked.

"I? No. My prince came in time," Mother had said.

I must always have known who the shell ladies were. Then if I loved her, why hadn't I been faithful to her? Why hadn't I given her the love and support she needed?

I walked all the way to the inlet. There fishermen were trying their luck and small boats sped in and out on the current. I stretched out on the sand and tilted the hat over my face, but the heat of the late morning sun was too suffocating to bear. When I started back, the sky was blue overhead and the clouds were towering snowy peaks on the horizon. My mind was mercifully blank. I found one shell worth picking up. It was orange, small and whelk shaped. I held it tightly as I walked, listening to my footsteps squeak in the sand and the lapping of the water, wondering whose spirit I was holding in my hand.

Chapter 8

To my relief I was on time for lunch, but as soon as I stepped into the garden, I heard Corallee screeching.

"You can't handle him yourself. And you got to get a male nurse for the nights or give him them drugs the doctor ordered. You can't do it yourself, and don't expect no more from me."

"Be quiet, Corallee. I know what I can and cannot do." Grandmother's voice shook despite the authority in her words.

The red gash on my grandfather's forehead explained their agitation. "What happened?" I asked.

"He got away from your grandma and took a tumble off the terrace steps while I was in the kitchen," Corallee said. "Lucky he didn't break his neck."

"Corallee, I've heard quite enough from you," Grandmother snapped. "If you can't hold your tongue, you can leave at once."

"And what'll you do without me, huh? Didn't the doctor say you got to take it easier? He said you'll kill yourself taking care of this old man who don't even know who's who no more."

"Charles knows very well who's who," Grandmother said. "He knows me. He's my husband and I'll take care of him. Now be quiet."

"There's the bell," Corallee said.

"I'll get it," I offered and ran to open the front door for the doctor, who was a short, self-confident looking man with a mustache. He followed me back to the garden where Grandfather was lying on the tile floor with a cushion from one of the lawn chairs under his head.

"How about if all you lovely ladies go inside while I examine my patient?" the doctor said. He got down on one knee beside the old man and applied a stethoscope to his chest.

"You sit down and I'll bring you a cup of tea," Corallee said to Grandmother. "Go on now. Kelly, you stay with your grandma."

Hesitantly I touched Grandmother's arm. To my surprise, she took my hand and held onto it. I led her into her sitting room to the comfortable armchair she favored. She sat heavily and leaned back closing her eyes.

"He was such a brilliant man," she said in a sorrowful voice. "Everyone admired him. At the club, even when the circulation in his legs got bad, we danced and people . . . He had such dignity."

I crouched beside her chair and stroked her hand to comfort her. "You must have loved him very much," I said.

"Charles and I—yes—we have loved one another. Even your father understood that my husband came first with me. Charles filled my life and your father knew—" She was silent, thinking. Then she said, "I have never understood why Harvey rebelled. He was such a quiet, obedient boy. We wanted him to go to Princeton as his father had. Charles moved mountains to get Harvey accepted despite his mediocre academic record. But, do you know, the day before Harvey was supposed to leave for freshman orientation—the very day before, he announced that he had joined the air force. It was a terrible blow to Charles. I was furious with my son, and as if he hadn't punished us enough, then he brought home a wife who was—well, hardly what we had hoped for for him."

"What did you have against my mother?" I asked, withdrawing my hand.

"Her background," Grandmother said. "She was four years older than your father and a widow. Harvey was a boy of twenty. What did he know about women? I told him if he chose to ruin his life that he mustn't expect help from us. That was my temper showing, and I've regretted my words. It gave her an excuse to separate him from us."

"But that's not true. Mother's the one who always said we should see you, but you made excuses. You said it wasn't convenient."

"You mother has never been a proper wife for my son. What does she have in common with him? She has neither breeding nor education. He only married her to punish us because I didn't pay him enough attention as a child. That was a fault in me, but I cannot help what I am." She looked at me directly. "Be glad you've inherited the Allgood constitution and not your mother's bad blood."

I jumped up, instantly regretting my sympathy

for her. "I don't care what you think of my mother," I said. "She's my mother and I love her."

"How much does she love you?"

"What do you mean?"

"Why do you think your father wouldn't let you see her the night she was taken to the hospital?"

"I don't know."

"Perhaps you should know then. Your mother swallowed enough sleeping pills so that she nearly didn't wake up."

"I hate you," I said.

"It doesn't matter how you feel about me. You're my granddaughter and I care about you. You have the potential to become all that we hoped your father would be—if you don't let your mother drag you down, that is."

"Where do you want me to set your tea?" Corallee asked with the tray in her hands.

"Mrs. Allgood?" the doctor called, appearing at the door behind Corallee. "I think if I get you a nurse, and we get him up to bed and keep him quiet for a day or two, he'll be all right. Nothing seems to be broken as far as I can tell."

My head was bursting with unfinished thoughts. One word kept spinning past me—suicide. That was what my grandmother had been telling me. But not my mother! My mother would never do that to me. She loved me too much to leave me that way.

I ran upstairs and, without being aware of what I was intending to do, went directly to the telephone on the night table beside my grandmother's canopied bed. I sat down on the ivory quilted bedcover and methodically proceeded to call the psychiatric unit at Mother's hospital. The nurse who answered had a voice that chimed. "I'd like to speak to Mrs. Allgood," I said.

"Who is this, please?"

"This is her daughter, Kelly Allgood. I have Dr. Bache's permission to speak to her," I lied.

I held my breath through the pause before the chiming voice answered uncertainly, "Well, I don't know. No one's around."

"The doctor said it would be all right," I urged her. "I'm calling from Florida. It's important."

"Well, let me see if she's up. Okay?"

It was the middle of the day. Could Mother be sleeping round the clock? I waited impatiently, excited now that I was finally going to hear her voice. All the vicious things my grandmother had said stopped stinging me. I was going to speak to my mother, my darling, wonderful mother who couldn't have, wouldn't have ever done what Grandmother said she'd done.

"Kelly?" the voice was breathy, hoarse as if she had just awakened.

"Mama," I said. "How are you? Are you getting better?"

"Kelly? Where are you?"

"In Florida, with Grandma. I wrote you a letter about it."

"Kelly, I wish—listen, honey, I can't talk to you. I don't feel very well."

"What's wrong?" I asked in alarm at the strange weakness in her voice.

"I'm afraid here, Kelly. I want to go home. Tell Daddy to make them send me home." Her voice was a child's whine. I couldn't believe it was Mother.

"Mother?"

"Tell Daddy," she said and there was a click that told me she'd hung up.

"Mother!" I screamed, and I stood there trembling and betrayed.

When I could move, I crept to my room and curled up in the armchair. I sat in the chair and wept until I'd emptied myself of tears. Then I stared out at the ocean, so big and eternal and alive with power. It calmed me to watch the ocean. It shrunk the enormity of my misery to human size. So my mother had tried to kill herself. She had gone crazy. She had lost control of her mind. The mother who had loved and cherished me all my life was gone and instead there was this hoarse-voiced creature who didn't care about me. She would never have tried to kill herself if she really loved me. She would have thought of me, and no matter how bad she felt, she would never never have wanted to leave me. She had no right. Nothing I had ever done deserved such punishment.

Hours later Corallee knocked on my door and said Grandmother was waiting and that I'd better get down to dinner fast. I got up unsteadily, feeling nauseated, took the first dress that came to my hand in the closet and changed into it.

Downstairs everything seemed normal again. "Your grandfather is resting," Grandmother said. "I'm sorry if what I said earlier upset you, Kelly. I was beside myself. Forgive me."

"I called my mother and spoke to her," I said. "I used your phone."

"And?"

"She's very sick."

"I'm sorry to hear that," Grandmother said. "I really am."

She sounded sincere, but her being sorry didn't matter to me at all. We discussed my using the phone without permission. Her rebuke was mild, just a request that I not do that again. When we'd done with the subject, I asked, "Are you going to get a night nurse for Grandpa?"

Grandmother sniffed. "I suppose I should try to find someone suitable. It's so difficult. I dislike having strangers in my house at night. It destroys one's sense of privacy."

I cut a piece from the veal cutlet and put it in my mouth. "This is tasty," I said, dutifully maintaining the conversation.

"Yes, Corallee does veal well. . . . Are you all right, Kelly? You don't look well."

"I think my stomach is upset or something," I said and stopped trying to pretend to eat. "May I be excused, please?"

"Tact has never been my strong suit," Grandmother said. "I wish I hadn't hurt you, Kelly."

"It's all right," I said. "I'm glad I know."

"Yes, knowing is best if one is strong enough to take it." Grandmother studied me with critical eyes as I left the room.

Chapter 9

"What your grandma ought to do is put him in a home. That's what she ought to do, but don't you tell her I said that. She'd have my head," Corallee said to me Friday morning of my first week in Florida. I had slept late and was getting my own breakfast in the kitchen where Corallee was busy setting up a tray of medicines, complete with a crystal pitcher of water, glasses and a silver spoon.

"Is he all right this morning?" I asked.

"Well, he had her up all night again."

"What do you mean?"

"Don't you know? He wanders. Spends the whole day in that chair like he can't move, but then won't stay put in bed at night. She's supposed to tie him down, but she don't like to do it. Once he got all the ways down to the beach before she caught him."

"Do you like my grandmother, Corallee?"

"Like her? What for? I got to eat and she pays my wages is all." She considered and then added, "Her and me get along okay. We got respect for one another."

Respect was important to both of them, I guessed, and maybe that was all they needed to have in common. Then I told Corallee I was off to the beach. I had a pain in my chest and a tangle of thoughts in my head. What I needed was someone to really talk to, and the only one possible was Evan. If nothing else, he could teach me courage. He had plenty.

For a change there were real waves, five feet high—big enough to crest and crash down with a satisfactory boom. But instead of sitting to watch the waves stretch their slippery bellies and swoop toward shore, I hurried to Evan's garden. Even the ocean couldn't heal me today. I needed to understand why my mother had tried to leave me before I could live with the knowledge that she had.

A trilling feminine laugh stopped me short just inside the wall. I stood hidden behind the sharp green spears of huge yucca plants whose centers were long stalks high as my head, topped with white flowers. The laugh ended in a catchy little hiccup. I could see the slender back of a delicate blond girl in a bikini. Evan, in bathing trunks with his misshapen legs exposed, was leaning across the breakfast table holding her hand. Even from the back of the garden, I could see the adoring way he was looking at her. He brought her hand palm up to his lips and murmured something that set off the trilling laugh again. The girl turned her head to brush at an insect on her shoulder, and I saw the outline of a lovely face. Was this his friend? But she was just a girl!

Hastily I backed out of the garden and returned

to the water's edge. Nothing was the way I expected it to be anymore. I couldn't count on anybody, not my mother or grandmother, not Evan either. I squatted and let the waves play tag with my toes. There in the foam was the hard edge of a big, white conch shell. I grabbed it before the surf took it away. The shell was broken, dull from being scoured by endless tumbling in the waves. It was not worth keeping except it seemed to have come right out of another of Mother's stories, the one about the princess Merry that went:

. . . Her stepmother hated her for her happy nature and cursed her to make all the events of Merry's life end in misery. Hoping to escape the curse, Merry married a good and powerful king. She bore a child, but the good king died and the child, who was the joy of Merry's life, wandered into the woods and was lost. In despair, Merry tried to drown herself. Then the king of the sea caught her dying spirit and placed it in a great white conch shell to protect it until the child should return to her. . . .

The back of the conch shell was broken out. It couldn't hold anything now, not even an unhappy spirit. I held it a minute before heaving it as far as I could, back into the waves. Let the sea take care of its own. I was no keeper of lost shell ladies. What did my mother want from me? She couldn't expect me to take care of her when she wouldn't even stay alive for my sake. I rubbed at my blistered, itchy nose and shivered. I was angry, too angry to care about anybody at that moment but myself.

I raced back over the deserted beach, panicking the sea gulls, which flew up from their orderly ranks to get out of my way. I had in mind to slather myself with suntan lotion and go for a long swim anyway, despite my painful sunburn.

"You just missed your grandma," Corallee said. "The chauffeur she gets Fridays took her and your grandpa to town for shopping. Serves you right for not getting back in time. They'll have lunch out and then they got a doctor's appointment to go to."

"She told me yesterday. I forgot."

"Well, you're just gonna be stuck here by your lonesome because I got the rest of the day off."

"Have a good time, Corallee."

"Going to. You behave yourself and don't get into no trouble now."

The water supported me like a foam-rubber pillow, only it was more yielding as I stroked my way through it. I swam parallel to shore, not very far out. If I started drowning, no king of the sea was coming to save me. Besides, being a spirit in a seashell wasn't my idea of a good life, not even a good afterlife. When I got tired, I rolled over and floated face up in the warm turquoise water. With my eyes slitted against the sun, I let the waves rock me.

Friend, I thought. Was that girl Evan's friend, the one he had said was coming? So much tenderness in the way he had kissed the palm of her hand. Could friendship be that tender? How would it be to love a crippled man? Already I could look at his legs without being disgusted, the way I could look at my grandfather now that I'd gotten used to his condition. And after the malformed legs stopped bothering me, then how would making love go? Awkward unless we were lying down. Then could his arms help him move? I could encircle him with my arms and hold him against me. He would need me to help him, but it would be clumsy, embarrassing to make love with a man who couldn't move around by himself. Yet the way he glowed when he looked at that girl had been beautiful. I imagined for a minute the glow had been for me, that his lips were on me. I was the delicate blond girl in his garden. Then I rolled over and swam for shore.

The air clung to me and the water dripping from my body was not sea water but perspiration by the time I entered the cool of my grandparents' house. The house was empty. I knew to whom I could talk if she'd accept a collect call from me—Bea Mayer, Mother's friend. The thought of confiding in someone gave me energy. It was one o'clock. Before Grandmother returned, right now—do it. I dialed the operator and gave her Bea's name and telephone number. Bea worked Saturdays at a rental firm. Today was her usual weekday off, but she might be out running errands. Be home, I prayed and was glad when Bea answered and accepted the charges.

". . . of course I know she's in the hospital, Kelly," she answered my first question. "I've been over there twice, but honey, they had her so drugged up that she didn't even know I was there. She's really out of it. I talked to her doctor and he says they're still experimenting to find what works best for her. Frankly, I think your father ought to try another doctor."

"I called her," I said, "and she didn't want to talk to me. She sounded awful."

"Well, she is suffering from a mental illness, Kelly. And all these drugs they're giving her

. . . Naturally, she's not going to sound like herself."

"Couldn't they just leave her alone? Why do they have to give her anything? Maybe if they just left her alone—"

"Your mother's a very sick lady. Face it, Kelly; she's been getting sicker and sicker. God, I'll never forget the day she called me and said she felt as if hot wax was dripping all over her. I rushed over and found her scratching herself so she had bloody streaks all up and down her arms. You were at school and your father was out of town—as usual. You didn't know about that time?"

"No, not exactly."

"Yes, she worked hard to hide it all from you, I know."

"Bea, is she crazy?"

"Not crazy insane—more like a nervous breakdown. She'll come out of it. She's a gutsy lady, your mother."

It sounded as if Bea didn't know about the overdose, and I wasn't about to risk her good opinion of Mother by telling her what Mother had tried to do to herself. I liked hearing that my mother was a gutsy lady though, and so I asked if she thought Mother was really getting well. Bea reassured me without really reassuring me, since I didn't know if she knew the whole story or not. Anyway, I thanked her and said how comforting it was to talk with her, but she interrupted me to say, "I'm glad to be of help, Kelly. You know I love your mother. But honey, the next time you need to talk, how about writing me instead and I'll write back. Okay?"

I winced. I knew calling collect was expensive. "Sure," I said. "Thanks again, Bea."

The mail slid through the slot in the panel next to the front door. I hung up the receiver and bent to pick up the three white envelopes and some throw-away advertising sheets from a local drugstore. To my delight, one of the letters was from Jennifer. I took shelter in my room in my favorite chair and curled up to read.

Dear Kelly,

You really had me scared. I couldn't figure out where you went and I thought maybe you and your mother got kidnapped or something because I kept calling and nobody was ever home. When your father called and told us what happened, I was so relieved. Well, my mother checked out the hospital right away, but she didn't find out much. I couldn't believe your mother's in the psychiatric unit. She's such an up sort of lady. What did she flip out over? I was going to visit her, but my mother said not to go. To be honest, I'm chicken about going to a psychiatric ward anyway. I know that's awful, but I'm being honest. Anyway, I'm going to leave some roses from our garden and a card at the desk for her, and I hope she gets well soon.

Now for the hot news. You really made an impression on Mark's cousin. After he got over the shock of how young you are, he started acting like he couldn't get you off his mind. Last thing he wrote Mark was that he might write you a letter soon. Of course, he just couldn't believe you're only fourteen. My mature friend! Are you breaking any hearts down there in Florida? I bet you are by now. In the meantime, your old friend Jennifer is going to have a ball when school's over, doing—you'll never guess what—helping Mark teach arts and crafts to underprivileged kids at a day camp. Of course,

I'm not being paid beans, but I'll love doing it, even though between baby-sitting my brother and seeing Mark and working during the day I'll be busy, busy, busy. Write and tell me how you're feeling, and don't worry about your mother. She'll get better. Write soon.

Love,
Jennifer

I finished the letter, disappointed that nothing in it touched me where I ached. She was talking to me about a boy who no longer mattered to me and dismissing the horror of what was going on with my mother as if it were minor. If my best friend didn't understand, who could I turn to? I felt as if I were alone on a raft drifting out to sea while everyone on shore looked the other way. The gardener to whom I'd been a stranger had come through for me, but nobody else had. My mother was crazy. She had tried to kill herself. I still needed her so much, but she wasn't there for me anymore.

The light had melted into late afternoon when I heard the front door open and voices, a man's reassuring rumble. "Easy now. There. We've got you home, Mr. Allgood." I rushed to the stairs and looked down.

"If you'll just help me get him to his room," Grandmother said to the man in the chauffeur's uniform, "once he's in his own bed, he'll be all right."

"What happened?" I asked as the trio made their slow way up.

"There, there, Charles," Grandmother said to her groaning husband. "You'll be upstairs in a minute." She was trying to support Grandfather on one side while the solidly built man, who still wore his visored cap, took most of the weight on the other.

I sidled down along the wall and asked, "Can I help?"

This time Grandmother looked at me. Her face looked like a head on a gravestone. "It was too much for him," she said. "I told that nurse in the doctor's office we couldn't wait—"

"Let me take Grandpa's arm. You're tired," I said.

"I'm fine." She wouldn't let go although she looked exhausted.

"I'll turn down his bed," I said and ran upstairs to do that. They entered the room in slow motion, barely making progress. "Shall I make some tea or soup or something?" I asked. There were silver-backed brushes on his dresser and a painting of Grandmother, gowned and bejeweled and beautiful, but the room smelled rancid.

"Soup would be nice if you can find something in the pantry," Grandmother said. She sat down suddenly on the lacquered valet chair that was meant to hold a suit so that it wouldn't wrinkle. The chauffeur finished guiding Grandpa to his bed. Grandmother closed her eyes and let her head fall back. I ran to her side and chafed her hands, frightened.

"Grandmother, are you all right? Shall I call the doctor?"

"I'm . . . fine. Just . . . a little tired."

I went to the bathroom between their two bedrooms and wet a facecloth with cool water. I tried to press it on her forehead, but she pushed my hand away and took the cloth saying, "Thank you, dear. Thank you." She touched the cloth to her eyes. I scurried down to the kitchen and poked around the pantry. The can of chicken-and-rice soup seemed appropriate. Then a pot and a can opener. When I finally located them, I couldn't figure out how to use the can opener and cursed my stupidity. I heard the front door close. The chauffeur had left. That meant I was alone in the house with two sick old people who were my responsibility. I steeled myself. I had to think clearly now. Should I call the doctor even though Grandmother had said not to? But I didn't know their doctor's name. As soon as the soup was hot, I poured it into two bowls and carried it up the stairs to Grandfather's room on a tray. Grandmother sat up stiffly when she saw me coming.

"How nice," she said. "That was kind of you to make the soup." She smiled. "I think you forgot the spoons though."

"Sorry," I said, feeling like an idiot. It occurred to me that I'd never had to take care of anybody else. Mother had always taken care of me. Never the other way around. I raced back down to the kitchen and this time remembered napkins too. When I brought them back up, Grandmother was sitting on the bed beside her husband putting damp cloths on his forehead.

"He's so exhausted, my poor darling. I don't know what I can have been thinking of to attempt so much today. . . . I bought you a present." She looked up at me. "I hope you like it. It's over there in my purse." Mystified, I brought the capacious canvas bag to the bedside to oblige her. It didn't make sense to me that she should have bought me a present.

"I thought you'd be angry with me because I wasn't here when you left this morning," I said.

"I was a little annoyed," Grandmother admitted. She looked more like herself already. She began feeding my grandfather his soup, blowing on each spoonful to make sure it wasn't too hot. "You seem to have a capacity for never being where one expects you to be at the right time, not an especially admirable trait I must say."

"I don't know why I'm always late down here. I'll try harder not to be," I said.

"Yes, well, I wanted to get you a sun hat of your own and a beach jacket, but nothing seemed appropriate for a young girl, so I bought you a trinket instead. See if you like it." She reached into the bag and came up with a small box.

I opened the box to find a thin gold chain with a tiny gold scallop shell hanging from it. For a moment I was frightened. Could she read my mind and know about the shell ladies? Coincidence? It could be. "It's lovely," I said sincerely. "So dainty. Thank you very much." Uncertainly I moved to kiss her, not sure she'd like to be kissed by me, but she smiled and offered her cheek.

"It suits you," she said with satisfaction. "And it's nice to get 'just because' presents, isn't it?"

"Very nice," I said. I used the mirror in the bathroom to catch the clasp. Grandmother was right. The small gold shell looked pretty lying in the hollow at the base of my neck. It did suit me, but why had she wanted to buy me a present when all I seemed to do was fight with her and irritate her? She had to know I didn't like her much. Did she like me anyway? I was her granddaughter, her only one.

I sighed. Life was so full of contradictions. What was I doing worrying about why my grandmother chose to buy me a gift now? That was the least important thing I had to think about. I went back to see what else I could do for them.

Chapter 10

I floated in the moonlight as if it, rather than the bed, was supporting my body and any minute I might be swept out the window into the night sky. The ocean sighed against the shore like an echo of my thoughts, all the regret and confusion that was keeping me awake. Even my dislike of Grandmother had gotten confused because I did admire her loyalty to her husband and she wasn't quite as rigid as I had thought. Evan had persuaded her to change her mind about the importance of keepsakes, and she had apologized to me for what she said about my mother. It touched me that she'd thought enough of me to give me that necklace, had picked it out with me in mind. Of course, she still didn't appreciate my mother. As a loyal daughter, I ought to go on hating Grandmother for that, but I didn't. I'm just not a good hater. I don't know if that's bad or good.

I thought of what Grandmother said about not putting my father first when he was a child. Had that changed him? Maybe he wouldn't have been such a solitary person if he'd been closer to his parents, or were people born with their personalities already set? I wondered if psychology books held the answers to questions like that. They were the kind of questions that intrigued me most. When I got to college, I could study psychology. I could even become a psychologist, maybe. I had never thought of that before. It pleased me to have a possible goal in mind for my future.

Sleepily, I tried to conjure up my mother. All I got was the faintest of shadows. She was so different now from the mother I knew. So much had happened to her. Bea said she'd been sick for a long time. That meant she had been changing right under my nose and I never noticed. As I thought about it, I dredged up remarks that should have caught my attention: "I take up too much space," she'd said to me, and recently she had said, "You don't need me any more, Kelly."

"Don't be silly," I'd answered and assured her that I did need her, and in any case, Dad needed her.

"Not the way I am," she said. "I've become so dull. I'm no fun anymore." I'd been impatient with Mother sometimes, impatient with having to say cheering things to her when I was eager to be off to Jennifer's house. I was so wound up in myself, expecting my mother to be a dependable part of the scenery.

I shuddered in the ocean-filled dark of Grandmother's guest bedroom. My mother had needed me, and I had deserted her long before she tried to desert me. If she had failed me by giving up the way she did, I had failed her first. I had no right to be angry with her. I was the one at fault. Except, what was so bad in her life that had depressed her so much? Just because I wasn't spending enough time with her? That wasn't enough to make her sick. It couldn't have been all my fault, and not all Dad's either. She should have built a better life for herself. She didn't have to be lonely. A daughter wasn't supposed to spend all her time with her mother and sacrifice her own life to make her mother happy. I love my mother, but I wouldn't love her for long if I could never leave her.

The humidity was so suffocating the next day that Grandmother ordered all the windows closed and turned on the air conditioning early. She settled down to read the morning paper aloud to Grandfather. Her pretense that he understood what he heard seemed to me not so much foolish as sad. I dragged myself through breakfast and then straggled down to the beach for my morning swim.

Even at ten, the sand was so hot that I had to run fast to reach the water. Then, just as I was about to plunge in, I heard someone hailing me.

"Kel—ly!"

I turned around and saw the slender blond girl waving at me. I stood waiting while she picked her way gingerly across the band of bleached sand to join me at the water's edge. As soon as I saw her up close, I realized that the "girl" was really a woman, a beautiful woman with fine lines just beginning to show around her eyes.

"Hello there. You are Kelly, then?" The voice was lilting, English, as lovely as the woman looked.

"Yes, I am."

"Evan said you were the only person I was likely

to meet on the beach in summer, though I did see a fisherman in a dune buggy last night." She held her hand out, and I shook it. "I'm Cynthia." The smile was girlish.

"You're Evan's friend?"

"Yes. I finally got here. Tell me, is the water full of Portuguese men-of-war and sharks and all manner of awful things as Evan has warned me?"

"I haven't noticed anything awful."

"Good. I thought he was being overly wary. I suspect he worries that he can't leap in and save me if I get into trouble."

"If you'd like to swim with me, I'll stay by you," I offered.

"Well, thank you. You are kind, but I understand you're a champion swimmer and I'm just a paddler. Please, don't let me delay you. I only wanted to ask if you'd come and see us this afternoon?"

"Oh, thank you. Yes, I'd be glad to."

"About three? I shall tell Evan that he's wrong. He thought my presence was what frightened you away."

"No," I said. "Not you at all, but I thought you might like to be alone with each other and so . . ."

"Ah, I see! You're very nice, Kelly. Evan said you were." She squeezed my hand. "Go and do your swim. I'll look forward to seeing you this afternoon."

Cynthia's smile put me in a better mood and I swam with pleasure. It was nice to have the visit to look forward to, a break in the monotony of the long, sultry day. Now that I'd met her, I felt silly thinking she was a girl. Hadn't Evan told me that his friend was a cardiologist? A doctor couldn't be that young. Funny to go visiting two adults as if they were friends. But down here, the age-group division was probably at fifty, with anyone under that being young.

I wore a pink shirtwaist. "Don't you look pretty!" Grandmother said. "Would you like to eat out tonight, Kelly? Your grandfather seems to be feeling well and Corallee is off today."

"That would be nice, Grandmother," I said. "I've been invited to Evan's house this afternoon. He has a friend staying with him. When do you want me back?"

"A friend?"

"Yes, a very pretty woman named Cynthia. I don't know her last name."

"Poor fellow," Grandmother said. "He'd so like to live a normal life."

"Maybe he will."

"Not likely. I wonder what she wants of him. Money, probably. I suppose he has enough to make it worth her while to overlook his limitations."

"Cynthia is a doctor. She doesn't need his money," I said in disgust. No sooner did I start liking Grandmother better than she said something awful. "And Evan's intelligent and interesting and brave. He's a wonderful man."

"Indeed," Grandmother said, "but no normal young woman, even a doctor, wants to tie herself to a cripple for life."

"That's cruel, Grandmother."

"Life is cruel. One needs strength to endure it."

I bit my lip to keep from arguing that one. "Will five be early enough?" I asked stiffly.

"Yes, five will do so long as you're on time."

I could feel my shirtwaist wilting in the wet heat

as I walked the short distance from the front door down the driveway to the street and along the high stone wall that hid Evan's house from the road. I pulled at one of the seahorse handles on the black iron gate and slipped through the opening. My shoes grated on the crushed-stone driveway as I walked to the arched doorway set back under a cavernous stone porch. I rang the bell. A lizard as long as my hand stood on the lip of a stone plant container, head raised, watching me. I stared back at it until Cynthia opened the door and it fled.

"There you are and how pretty you look," Cynthia said. "You make me ashamed I didn't change for tea." She wore a gauzy shirt over her bikini. Her fair skin was burnished by the sun.

"Pretty? I'm peeling all over," I said. "*You* didn't get too much sun, did you?"

"Oh, never. I use scads of sunscreen and then I only stay out a few minutes. I'd gone inside long before you got back from your swim this morning. You really are a good swimmer."

"Thank you."

"Come along then. I need you to be on my side. Evan's been teasing me unmercifully."

She led me through the entry hall that was even more grand than my grandparents'. Again my eyes were dazzled with gold leaf and the gleam of marble.

"Here's Kelly, Evan," Cynthia sang. "I hope you left her some biscuits and didn't eat up all the chocolate ones yourself."

"Listen to her," Evan said, wheeling over to an open bar in the glass-enclosed porch. The rattan furniture surprised me after the antique elegance of the main part of the house. "She's trying to get back at me because I pointed out how odd it is for a woman with her intelligence not to understand time differences between the U.S. and England. Now I ask you, Kelly, isn't that a simple time concept?"

"Not to me."

"Of course not," Cynthia said. "Nobody but a lawyer could possibly remember whether it's five or six hours earlier or later in England."

"So she woke her children from their nap and they were crabby and that upset her."

"Well, one does want to be missed a teeny bit when one's a mother, wouldn't you say?"

"Are you really a mother?" I asked. "When I first saw you, I thought you were a girl near my age."

Evan laughed. "So you suspected I was a cradle robber, did you, Kelly?"

"No, I didn't. I just didn't know . . . How old are your children, Cynthia?"

"My little boy is three and my girl is almost five. Their granny's come to stay with them in London while I'm here on holiday with Evan. I've never been away from them so long before. It's quite difficult—for me if not for them."

"I'm sure they miss you."

"Do you think so? They don't sound as if they do when I ring. They're full of all the lovely things Granny's doing with them. I think they may decide to dismiss me in favor of Granny before long."

"How could they possibly not miss the most adorable mother any child could have?" Evan said.

"Evan! Don't embarrass me in front of Kelly. She'll think we're absurd."

"We are a little, aren't we?" He grinned and took her hand and put the drink that he'd just made into it. "Have a sip of this," he said, "and forget your jealousy of Granny."

"If he isn't teasing me, he's embarrassing me," Cynthia said. "You must help us to behave better, Kelly."

"Nonsense. We're on vacation. We can behave any way we please," Evan said. "Kelly, what may I offer you? Punch or soda or tea with the cookies, or 'biscuits,' as Cynthia calls them?"

"Punch would be nice," I said. I sat down on a chair that looked like a throne with a high round back and stared admiringly at Cynthia.

"What do you do with yourself here all day besides swim?" Cynthia asked me.

"I read a lot and sleep a lot and try to fit into my grandparents' routines."

"It's lucky she's so self-sufficient," Evan said. He stopped his chair next to mine and handed me my punch then he turned his gaze on Cynthia as if just looking at her gave him pleasure.

"It must be very dull for you here," Cynthia continued to me.

"I'm here because my mother's in the hospital and my father doesn't want me staying in our house alone. If my mother gets well, I'll go home."

"If?"

"She's very ill." I hesitated. Cynthia was a doctor. "She's depressed," I blurted out. "I don't understand what that means really."

"I'm not a psychiatrist," Cynthia said. "All I know about is hearts, not heads, but . . . Have you spoken to your mother's doctor? He should be able to explain it to you."

"I haven't spoken to anybody except Evan. Grandmother says if my mother wants to, she can make herself well. Is that true?"

"Depression is an illness," Cynthia said—just

what Evan had told me. "At least severe depression, the kind that lands you in a hospital is. It's not like feeling down for a while the way we all do now and then. It's like having pneumonia or getting stones in your kidney. You need professional help to get well—drugs and other kinds of therapy a doctor can prescribe."

"And will she get well? Do people always get over it?"

Cynthia hesitated and looked at Evan. "Kelly's asking your medical opinion, Cynthia," Evan said. "I think she wants to hear the truth."

I glanced at his handsome profile, hoping I was as brave as he imagined.

"You really need to speak to your mother's psychologist, Kelly," Cynthia said. "He or she is the one who can best tell you what to expect. I don't know much more about depression than a well-read lay person, actually. It's not my field. All I can tell you is that more people in this country are supposed to be suffering from depression than from any other mental ill and women are more prone to it than men. Mostly people do recover. A friend of mine was back to her normal self in six months. I believe people can recover in less time—or more."

"And being left alone?" I asked. "Could being alone a lot cause depression?"

"Cause it? I doubt that," she said. "I suspect there needs to be something more traumatic in one's life to precipitate depression, but I don't know for sure. I've read that many women suffer an empty-nest syndrome, that is they feel useless when they don't have someone to take care of, and feeling useless or worthless leads to depression. Is your father gone from home?"

"He's away a lot because of his job," I said. "But I was home—not as much as I used to be though."

"For heaven's sake," Cynthia said, "whatever you do, don't blame yourself. You're not responsible for your mother's being ill. You have nothing to feel guilty about."

"But I didn't spend as much time with her as she liked."

"Of course not. A girl your age is supposed to spend time with her friends. That's part of growing up and becoming independent, which is what you're supposed to do in the normal course of your development into adulthood." She wrinkled her nose and turned to Evan. "Am I sounding too awfully stuffy?"

"To me you sound fine," Evan said.

I took a deep breath and said, "To me too. You've helped me a lot." There was more I wanted to ask her, but that would mean revealing more about my mother than I should. What she had tried to do—I couldn't talk about that to someone who didn't know her. I let the conversation shift to lighter things, to beach experiences and funny vacation mishaps we had had. They told me how they'd met at a party on one of Evan's frequent visits to London. In no time it was five o'clock and I jumped up to leave.

"If I'm late again, Grandmother will kill me."

"Come again," they said as if they meant it. "Come as often as you like."

I felt lighter going back. Some weight had been lifted from me. I couldn't explain it unless it was my guilt that I had left behind.

Chapter 11

July was the longest month of my life. I had never known days as endless, even though I invented routines for myself to pass the time. In the morning I swam and then there was lunch and the daily letter writing, always to my mother, sometimes to Jennifer and occasionally to my father who even wrote me back, letters that must have come hard to him. I could just see him sitting with pen in hand trying to think of what to say. He described political conditions in some of the cities he had flown to and gave me detailed weather reports, nothing about the people with whom he worked, not even the copilot he flew with who was his friend. He called me during those days when he got home and spent his time visiting Mother in the hospital. No progress there, he said. He promised to try to see me soon.

Jennifer's letters were mostly about her experiences at the playground where she was teaching. She loved the kids but sounded bored with Mark.

He was possessive. He had too good an opinion of himself. He had a concave chest. She said she missed me, and I certainly missed her too, but the constricted life of my grandparent's household seemed more real to me than the experiences my mother and father and Jennifer were having. They seemed very far away. Mother never answered my letters. I didn't even know if she was getting them. I didn't try to call her again. Since talking to Cynthia, I'd become less anxious about her. I began to accept what Grandmother said, that Mother was getting good care, and there was nothing I could do to speed her recovery except wait patiently.

Evan presented me with a box of the most gorgeous shells, fit palaces for shell ladies. They had been his mother's and were store bought, collected from places like the South Seas and the Philippines. I now owned an apple-sized turban shell that looked as if it were made of pearl, and a delicate chambered nautilus with brown and white spots, as well as a huge triton trumpet shell. Sometimes, before I fell asleep at night, I'd make up my own shell lady stories from fragments I remembered my mother telling me and bits of my own invention.

. . . Through the castle window she could see off into the distance in every direction as far as the borders of lands very different from her own. Each had a special color and design. One was misty, and one was mountainous and dark, and one shimmered in rainbows. Another was a cliff of ice. Whenever travelers came to the castle, the princess asked them about the lands they had traveled through, and from listening, she learned the customs and language of these strangers. She begged the king who was her father to let her travel to these wondrous places, but he would never let her go, not until she had married and had a husband to protect her.

One day the longing to see distant lands came over her so strongly that she hailed a knight on a swift black stallion and begged him to carry her off with him. When her father found out, he was so angry that he banished her from his castle forever.

Well, the knight took her away, but he was soon killed in battle and the princess was stranded. She wandered alone to the edge of the sea, and suffered cold and hunger and despair until the king of the sea rescued her spirit and placed it in a turban shell made of glistening pearl. There she waited forever while the world came and went around her. . . .

The only whole shells on the beach were tiny pink or white coquinas that looked like babies' fingernails. I remembered my mother finding small pointed drill shells in the surf, but I couldn't find any. Mostly I swam and read and forgot about shell ladies.

"Your father called. He's going to be at the West Palm Beach airport for a few hours and wants you to meet him for lunch at a restaurant near there," Grandmother informed me when I came in from the beach one day.

"When?"

"Tomorrow, Kelly. I've ordered a taxi for you."

"Really?" I was pleased but wary. "He must want to see me for some reason. Is something wrong with Mother? Is she worse?"

"Good heavens, child, you worry too much for a

girl your age. He didn't say a word about your mother."

"Did you ask?"

"There's no need to be rude," she said. "He would have mentioned it if there'd been any change." She was annoyed with me, so I apologized for challenging her.

The next morning I dressed in my pink shirtwaist because lunch with my father was an event. Grandmother looked me up and down while I waited for the taxi.

"No stockings?" she asked.

"I never wear stockings in the summer."

She shook her head over that, but said only, "You're graceful, Kelly. You have the look of a thoroughbred."

I laughed.

"What's funny?" she asked, frowning at me.

"Good thing I like horses," I teased, "otherwise it's not a very flattering comparison." To my surprise, she laughed too. Then she gave me money for the taxi and sent me on my way. I sat up straight in the back of the cab feeling terribly sophisticated. I'd never been invited to lunch alone with my father before.

We left the shaded streets of private homes behind and sped down a four-lane highway that was flat and bordered by oversized signs grabbing for our attention. The only time highways ever look pretty to me is at night when it's raining and all the colors run in jagged ribbons of light on the slick road.

In less than half an hour, we drew up to the paneled double doors of Mickey's Steak House. I saw Dad waiting there for me and forgot to pay the fare in my eagerness to hug him. Dad took care of the driver, then gave me a kiss in return for the stranglehold I had on him. I hadn't realized how much I'd missed my parents until that moment. Dad was as tanned as I was, not unusual since he spends most of his time lying around pools at hotels, reading while he waits for his bosses to need him. It's good he's such a patient man. He looked as tall and thin and serious as ever, but what he said to me was, "You've changed."

"I have?"

"You look grown up and very pretty," he said.

Two compliments in one day! My head was going to turn. I glanced at myself in the mirror as we passed through the hall into the main dining room. My hair was messed up. My dress hung unevenly and was creased from the car. Obviously my father didn't see me too clearly.

Inside, the restaurant was dark and over airconditioned. The hostess seated us at a table where we could look at a bubbling fish tank with fancy-tailed goldfish swimming about in an undersea green. Dad ordered a Scotch on the rocks for himself and a Bloody Mary without the vodka for me, a Virgin Mary the waitress called it. I shivered.

"Want my jacket?" Dad asked.

"No thanks, I'm fine. This is nice. I mean having lunch with you and all. Have things been going okay for you, Dad?"

"Fine," he said. "The normal hurry up and wait. I finish a book a day and do my laps in the pool. Rough life, huh?"

"You're going to run out of spy stories one of these days," I teased.

"Then I might be forced to read something educational." He smiled his homely smile at me.

We ordered lunch from the cheerful, gray-haired waitress, steak for Dad and stuffed shrimp for me. As we walked over to the salad bar, a long, fully laden table under a hooded hanging light fixture, I asked, "Dad, do you remember Evan Stone?"

"The crippled fellow? What about him?"

"He and I became friends this summer," I said, and because I didn't like hearing Dad label Evan the same way Grandmother had, I added, "He's a terrific person."

"Is he? I didn't know him very well."

Dad took a serving forkful of salad greens and spooned some blue cheese dressing over it, then waited while I filled my plate with a sampling of everything. Rabbit food was what Dad called salad. His idea of a good meal was steak and a baked potato.

"Evan says you saved his life," I said.

"I pulled him out of a pool once, but we were never friends."

"You didn't like him?"

"I didn't know him, Kelly."

Because Evan can't walk, I thought as we threaded our way past the other diners to our table next to the fish tank. My father had no more tolerance of physical or mental problems than my grandmother did. If a person wasn't healthy, they were weak and therefore worthless. Grandpa was an exception to that, of course. I wondered if Dad would make an exception of Mother, if he loved her enough. Or was he going to leave her one of these days the way all her shell ladies got left? Her stories had always had the ring of truth. Maybe

Mother had been afraid all these years that he might leave her someday. How strange life was. I knew so little about the one person I'd been sure I knew best.

Dad kept playing with the ice cubes in his glass as he said, "I've changed your mother's doctor. The one she had didn't seem to be making any progress. Now we have a team, a psychiatrist, a psychologist, and a social worker. The psychologist is a woman with a reputation for getting people on their feet again. Dr. Sarah Landsberg is her name."

"Does she think Mother can be cured?"

"She won't promise anything. Your mother hasn't responded to treatment yet. If nothing happens soon, maybe we'll try another treatment center."

"When I called her a few weeks ago, Mother sounded scared about being in the hospital," I said. "She didn't sound like herself at all."

"That's the drugs. They mix her up." He sealed his lips as if the subject pained him, but he was the one person from whom I didn't have to hide anything, and I needed some answers, so I probed further.

"Dad, I know what happened that night. Grandmother let it slip."

"She told me. She regrets that."

"I'd rather know the truth. I hate not knowing what's going on with my own mother."

He frowned into his glass instead of looking at me. "I thought it was better for you not to know."

"I'm a lot more mature than you think I am, Dad."

"Maybe," he said, "but that's not necessarily so good. It's not good to grow up too fast."

"About Mother—" I said.

"Yes."

"Tell me why she did it."

"Wait a second!" He fixed his eyes on me and said earnestly, "Your mother took too many pills. She isn't sure herself whether she just got confused or whether she did it deliberately."

"Dad, why do you want to fool yourself?"

"I am telling you what your mother says. She doesn't want to believe that she'd try to do away with herself. She feels guilty even thinking that she might have done that to us. It would be a terrible way to fail as a wife and mother, do you see that?"

I nodded. A muscle in Dad's cheek twitched, and he dropped his eyes to hide the pain in them from me. I'd never seen my father hurting. Gently, I asked, "Was it you or the doctor who didn't want me to see Mother in the hospital, Dad?"

"Both of us. Your mother was so far gone. She wouldn't have known you were there, and it would have been a terrible way for you to remember her."

"Do you think we failed her?" I asked.

"What do you mean?"

"We left her alone a lot, you and I," I said.

"The psychiatrist says her depression could be a chemical imbalance in her body, or—he said it could be a delayed reaction to her childhood," Dad explained carefully. "Your mother had a rough time as a kid. The way Sarah Landsberg—she's the psychologist—puts it is that a bad background can make you feel you're not worthwhile. So it sets you up for a depression later on in life."

"I know about her childhood," I said, wondering if I did know, and asked, "Like how was it rough?"

"Like her father didn't believe she was his child because she was dark and everybody else in the family was blond, and her mother knocked her around a lot and blamed her for everything that went wrong. You know, she ran away when she was sixteen and went to work as a waitress."

"And she dropped things on all the guys from the air force base who came into the diner, and they teased her. I know; she told me that part. That was where she met her first husband." Mother hadn't told me about her father not accepting her though, or that her mother had abused her. "Was her first husband nice?" I asked.

"Daniel?" Dad's voice brightened. "He was older, kind of a father figure to your mother. He was my friend too. She had a rough time of it when he got killed—his plane took a nose dive on takeoff."

"But you fell in love with her even though she was four years older than you."

"Honey, I was the oldest twenty-year-old in existence, and your mother was the most lively, lovable girl I'd ever met."

"And you still love her?"

"Sure I do."

"That's good to hear," I said. I finished my shrimp, too busy thinking to taste what I was eating, and then I dared to ask, "Dad, if you love Mother, why couldn't you spend more time at home so she wouldn't be so lonely?"

"You mean change my job? I offered to do that when a desk job came up a while back. Your mother said she didn't want me to give up flying. I'm a limited sort of man. Flying's the only thing I'm happy doing."

"Then how's she going to get well?"

"She's got to get well for her own sake, honey. She's got to find strength to live for herself like everybody does eventually."

"And you don't think we're guilty for not giving her enough?"

"Neither of us can be her crutches," he said. "No, we're not guilty."

With a pang of recognition, I suddenly remembered another of Mother's shell lady stories.

. . . Once there was a little princess born into a family of blue-eyed, tow-haired people, but the princess was dark haired and her eyes weren't blue, but brown as mud, and her father hated her from the moment she was born and would never let her ride on his shoulders like her brothers and sisters. And her mother slapped her even when she hadn't done anything wrong, and her sisters made fun of her turned-up nose and curly hair and blamed all their mischief on her. When the little girl was old enough, she left home and got herself a job and tried very hard to please everybody. But she never believed people when they told her they loved her although she wanted very much to believe them.

One day a man with the kindest face in the world came and said he would take care of her forever. This man she believed, and for a while she woke up filled with joy every morning and went to bed smiling every night, and she laughed and laughed to make up for all the laughter she had missed as a child. Then one day the man with the kindest face in the world left her. The girl had nothing more to laugh about. So she took her tears to the seashore to mix with the sea's salty water, but when she tried to drown herself, the king of the sea wouldn't let her drown. He bore her spirit back to shore and said she could live in the shell he gave her and bake in the sunlight and roll in the briny waves and be admired by all. . . .

Mother, I thought, my shell lady mother! She had always been so full of fear, and who was the king of the sea and why wasn't he saving her?

Over dessert, my father finally got around to what he'd wanted to see me about. "Listen, Kelly, the fact is, you're going to have to get along without your mother for a while which means we've got to make some plans for your future. Fall is almost here, and the fact is—you won't be able to go home. You can either stay with your grandmother and go to school down here or go away to a boarding school."

"A boarding school? What kind of boarding school? Where?"

"I'm researching that. I've heard about a couple of schools that sound pretty good."

"I'd hate boarding school."

"Why?"

"Because I wouldn't know anyone."

"Well, you could stay here. Your grandmother says you're welcome, but I do know people who've gone to boarding schools and liked them. The fact is, I went to one. You'd be among people your own age, at least."

"I don't want to stay with my grandparents," I said quickly, "but why can't I go home and go back to my regular school? Other girls my age get their own meals and clean up after themselves. I'm a responsible person."

"No, honey. You can't live alone. It's out of the question with me away so much."

"You could hire a housekeeper, couldn't you, for what boarding school would cost?"

"Kelly, your mother probably won't even be at a hospital near home, if you're thinking you could see her. As for the cost, your grandmother's offered to help with it."

"She'll do anything to get rid of me," I said.

"Are you sure that's fair?"

"No," I admitted.

"There's a school in Albany that's supposed to be good," he said, "I think it's coed. Possibly you could visit your old school friends from there. Want me to get an application and some literature from them?"

"I don't care," I said, and then I thought of Jennifer. Albany was only half an hour from Schenectady. "If it was that close, it might not be so bad," I said.

Dad looked relieved. He talked a little more about boarding school. He made it sound as if all he'd done there was sports with a few hours of study mixed in for balance. I asked him if he'd made any friends. "Not many," he said. His childhood had probably not been too happy either, I guessed. I'd been luckier than either of my parents.

Somehow on my way back in the taxi, I felt good, with a better appetite for the future than I'd had in months. Even the idea of boarding school seemed exciting. I'd be with kids my own age. I'd make friends, maybe even manage to see Jennifer if I went to school in Albany. And Mother would get well, and I'd see her again. I wasn't guilty and neither was my father. If anyone was at fault, it was my mother for letting herself break down the way she had. She should have gotten help sooner. She owed that much to Dad and me. I felt young and free and pleased with myself. Even my reflection in the rearview mirror of the taxi looked pretty.

Chapter 12

The sense of well-being I'd gained from my lunch with my father lasted as August began. No more gnawings of guilt. In the fall I'd go away to school and make a brand-new beginning. I'd stop being a loner and become somebody else, a friendlier, more social somebody. There was nothing I could do to make my mother well. She wasn't my responsibility after all.

Daydreams as fragile and intriguing as soap bubbles filled my waking hours. I'd take off on something like the adoring look Evan had given Cynthia, a look that could have been an advertisement for love, and I'd imagine a boy who would look at me that way and what he would say and what I would answer and where we would go together. Whole sagas of romance worked themselves out in my head. Most had happy endings.

Evan and Cynthia had both gone back to their respective jobs, but Evan expected to return for a few more days of finishing up, and had promised me I'd see him then.

One afternoon a fierce wind rattled the palm leaves. I had seen spray flying off the tops of shoulder-high waves on the beach that morning. "Storm's coming," Corallee said as she passed Grandmother's sitting room. According to the newspaper, a hurricane had skirted the edge of Jamaica, Grandmother reported, and we were getting the effects of it. For a while I watched the woolly gray clouds shepherded together by bullying wind. I expected a really dramatic confrontation between sea and sky, but the wind calmed and all we got was heavy rain. The rain shattered the sky when it came and smacked against the roof, narrowing our breathing space. Thunder cracked and menaced.

"I feel as if I'm under water," I said to Grandmother as I looked out her sitting-room window at the torrent of gray water.

"It'll stop soon," Grandmother said. "Do you ever play Scrabble, Kelly?" Grandpa was upstairs napping, apparently undisturbed by the storm.

"Mother and I play a lot," I said.

"Your grandfather and I used to play. Would you care to have a game with me?"

She turned out to be a formidable opponent. Mother and I are about equal in skill, but my grandmother beat me every time. Our Scrabble games became a daily challenge that I enjoyed. Grandmother gave me pointers, like to save useful letters and go for seven-letter words. She rarely made a score under three hundred, but when I finally managed to win a game, she acted as proud of me as I was of myself. Besides that, she was a gracious winner. Playing Scrabble with her made me like her better.

One morning Grandmother invited me to go into town with her. "Your grandfather needs a haircut. People will mistake him for a poet at the rate his hair is growing." She brushed his thick mane behind his ears in a fond gesture, apparently not seeing that with his mindless stare nobody could mistake him for anything but what he was. Her tenderness toward him touched me.

"We should also start shopping for your school clothes, Kelly. You can't go off with last year's wardrobe," she continued, though I hadn't answered her invitation.

"Sure I can," I said. "I'm still the same size and I have plenty of clothes."

"Nonsense. A girl your age can never have too many clothes. A new school should be the occasion for a shopping expedition."

"Let's wait," I said. "I don't really feel like shopping for fall things when it's so hot." Having seen the stores Grandmother shopped in, I couldn't imagine finding anything appropriate for a girl my age or for a northern climate. Besides, shopping for school clothes was something my mother and I always did together. It seemed disloyal to go with anyone else.

Grandmother didn't try to force me. Lately, she had been less domineering. She no longer found fault with me. When our opinions differed, instead of dismissing mine, she'd discuss the subject. True, neither of us changed our minds, but we weren't getting angry with each other either. We were getting along better.

After my grandparents left in the limousine, I

decided to check and see if Evan had returned. This was the week he'd said was most likely. Nobody was in his garden. I stood at his terrace door, knocked and called his name. At first, I thought the house was empty. Then I heard his wheelchair rolling on the polished floors.

"Kelly!" he said, "I was just about to call you. You must have ESP." His smile was only half the wattage he'd been giving out when Cynthia was around.

"Something wrong?" I asked.

"Do I look as if something's wrong?"

"Sort of."

"Women!" he said in chagrin. "You can always tell, can't you?"

"I don't know," I said, noting that he'd avoided mentioning what was wrong.

"Well, come on in. I'm working in the kitchen. It's the last room I have to do, thank God. You can help me decide whether I like the family Wedgwood well enough to hang on to some of it."

I walked behind him into the enormous, high-ceilinged kitchen, which had glass-doored cabinets all around it and a butcher-block counter in the center of the floor. He had stacked dishes and vases and serving platters and silver all over every horizontal surface. "What a mess," I said.

"Isn't it?"

"How is Cynthia?"

"Fine, I expect. Last I heard."

"Oh." So that was why he looked down. "It didn't work out?"

"No. I'll see her in London though." His lips smiled but his eyes didn't. "She's a marvelous woman, isn't she, Kelly?"

"I guess so. I didn't get to know her all that well."

"Well, take my word for it," he said. "She's one terrific lady."

"I'm sorry you're not going to marry her," I blurted out. He turned white, then red. "I'm sorry," I repeated. "I know it's none of my business."

"Was I that obvious?" he asked.

"Well . . ."

He sighed. "She did consider it, but, as she told me, she has too many other commitments—to her children and her work. She claims she can't give me enough, and it's true, a relationship can't be all one way. You've got to give as well as get. Perhaps when she's had longer to recover from her divorce . . . Who knows?" He smiled.

He was so gallant I couldn't stand it. "She shouldn't have turned you down. You're the one who's marvelous," I said.

"Well, thanks. I can use a vote of confidence right now," he said.

"Maybe she'll change her mind."

"Not likely, but we're still friends, she and I. Listen, I'm lucky just to have her as a friend. I'm lucky in a lot of things. Most of what I've wanted out of life, I've gotten—not without a struggle, sure, and not without disappointments, but I'm doing fine, Kelly. I'm basically a lucky guy."

"How can you say that? You don't really mean it."

"Yes, I do. Listen, I've had the love and support of a bunch of people—my parents, other relatives, friends. I've always had a rooting section behind me. That's the important thing in life—love and support."

I thought of my mother and my heart sank. The only love and support she'd ever had in her life had been from my father and me. Who was going to give her the courage to get well if we weren't there beside her when she needed us? Long-distance love was like Jennifer's letters, mostly off the mark.

"Well," Evan said. "Shall we go to the beach and feed the sea gulls, or do you want to help me pack and label this mess of stuff?"

"Pack and label," I said and was glad because he turned out to be fun to work with. As I handed him dishes, which he wrapped in newspapers and stored in cartons, he told me stories about parties his parents had had and the silly things distinguished people had said or done. There was a scientist who sat down to dinner with his pet falcon on his shoulder and the South American ambassador who dropped his false teeth in the soup. Evan made his parents sound a little foolish but very lovable.

The afternoon went by too fast, but he pleased me at the end of it when he asked if I'd write and tell him what was happening in my life. "Sure I'd like to. Will you write me back?" I asked.

"I certainly will. Can't think who'd make a better pen pal than you, Kelly." He took a sheet of paper from the clipboard on the table and wrote his New York address in a handwriting as bold as his smile. "Whenever you get down to the big city, give me a call and I'll take you out to lunch."

"That would be nice," I said. "Are you leaving soon?"

"Afraid so. Your grandma's favorite chauffeur is taking me to the airport after I sign some papers at the bank tomorrow morning."

"So this is good-bye," I said sadly.

He held out his hand. "You're a delightful girl, and I know things will come out right for you."

I was too choked up to say anything. Instead of shaking his hand, I put my arms around him and hugged him. He seemed surprised, but then he hugged me back and kissed my cheek. I raced back to Grandmother's. Love and support, he had said. The most important thing is love and support. The words flew inside me like banners in the wind.

Chapter 13

I had taken over the feeding of Evan's sea gulls. Although I never trusted them too close to me, I liked to watch them swoop over the water to pluck out bait fish that were invisible to me. It was amusing to see them bump each other from favored spots according to their status in their social order, as if one spot was better than another. They reminded me a little of my grandmother, handsome and strong but not altogether endearing.

Not so long after Evan left, I got a letter from Mark's cousin, Gerry. It was a funny letter, full of remarks about how he couldn't understand why a mature, practically adult male like him should be interested in a mere baby such as me. He guessed I must have a mysterious charm, and would I write and tell him what I'd thought of him. I realized how much growing up I'd done during the summer when I found myself writing him back in a teasing way. "Don't worry, Gerry. I think seventeen is too young to be accused of being a dirty old man," I said. I wrote him about Evan too, and about how I was looking forward to going away to boarding school. I even gave him the address in case he wanted to write me there. No question I'd matured enough to handle Gerry now. I didn't write him about what had happened to my mother. She was bedded down in a back room of my mind. All the sunshine was in the front room where I was living.

One day a week into August, Corallee headed me off as I entered the garden from the beach. "Your grandma's got company," she hissed at me. "You better dress like a lady for lunch today. Go upstairs the front way so they don't see you running around barefoot and naked."

"Yes, ma'am," I said. "Any other orders, Corallee? Want me to wear a bra too?"

"Don't you mouth off to me. I got enough trouble."

I caught her arm before she scuttled off. "Who's the company?"

"Old friends from way back back before your grandpa got sick. They been around the world. They're the family built the pavilion in the hospital where my sister had her gallbladder."

"I didn't know you had a sister."

"I got a sister, got a mother too at home, and four nephews and a grandniece."

"That's nice, Corallee. I'll put on a dress."

"You do that."

Dear Corallee! I wondered if she was as grouchy with her family as she was here. Probably. Grouchiness was the basic ingredient of her personality. I put on the inevitable pink shirtwaist and combed my hair. The girl in the mirror did look older, sixteen at least and vivid, the way my mother was vivid, even though my nose isn't much and my eyes are too narrow.

The old couple Grandmother introduced me to in the garden were nowhere near as distinguished as my tall, spare grandmother. The woman was dumpling shaped with beady blue eyes and the man sat hunched behind a huge beak of a nose.

"Now where have you been hiding this young beauty all these years?" the woman, Mrs. Clarendon, said when I had settled onto a cushioned garden chair. I blushed, which must have been the approved response, because Mr. Clarendon turned triumphantly to Grandma and continued, "What you ought to do is take this granddaughter of yours with you somewhere. Did you ever make that trip to Kashmir you used to talk about?"

"No, Emma. We've not been traveling much in recent years," Grandmother said.

"Much, huh! You've immobilized yourself here with Charles. You have some kind of a martyr complex, and it's not the least bit becoming, not the least."

"Don't exaggerate, Emma. I chose not to travel anymore, that's all."

"I'm not exaggerating, and you know it. Now you answer this—"

"Emma, calm yourself," her husband said, but she brushed him away with a gesture of her hand.

"Just tell me this," she continued to Grandma, "if Charles still had his wits about him, would he want you to bury yourself here in this house with him? Would he?"

"Emma, you are getting to be a busybody in your old age," Grandmother said. "Isn't she, Cyril?"

"That's not old age. Emma's always been a busy-body."

"Just answer me and I'll shut up. Because I know that if Charles knew what you were doing to yourself he'd be furious with you."

"You're wrong, Emma. Charles would understand."

"What? It makes no sense your giving up all your activities. You're turning yourself into an old woman, and what for? He doesn't even know."

"He knows," Grandmother said. "And I know."

I was impressed with my grandmother's dignity, but half-convinced that Emma was right. It was like listening to a debate when both sides sounded right. "You don't even see your old friends," Emma went on querulously.

"Most of them are dead, except for you and Cyril, and I do see you here in my garden, do I not?" Her tone was so chilly it would have silenced me, but Emma pushed on.

"Nonsense. Why, I met Martha Worth and she thought you were dead. It's unhealthy. Wrong, wrong, wrong for you to cut yourself off in your prime."

"Cyril!" Grandmother begged, and now she looked distressed. "Do make her hush. Tell me about your trip, why don't you? I'd so looked forward to hearing. I understand you took the Trans-Siberian Railway?"

Emma subsided with a sigh and Cyril began a long droning description of what sounded like the most uncomfortable train ride in the world. As a travel agent, he would have convinced me to stay home. He was still going on when Corallee said lunch was served. Grandmother put her hand on

my grandfather's shoulder. He whoofed and then
rose, looking at her in bewilderment. She led him to
the table and settled him in his place.

"I hope you don't mind eating this early," Grandmother said to her guests, "but this is the time
Charles is used to. Routines are so comforting as
one gets older, don't you think?"

At lunch Emma drew me out, and I found myself
confiding my joy in swimming and my pleasure in
reading *Great Expectations*. Her favorite reading,
Emma confessed, was "those dreadful love stories."
She gobbled them up by the pound and read them
until long after midnight on nights when she
couldn't fall asleep.

"Still dreaming some handsome fellow's going to
sweep her off her feet one of these days," Cyril said
and guffawed.

Next Emma entertained me with the story of
how she had met her husband by tripping him in the
dining room of the Breakers Hotel in Palm Beach.
She'd been there with her parents.

"That was fifty years ago," she said and dimpled.
I liked Grandmother's friends. They were lively
company, and I was sorry to hear they were on
their way to New York and we wouldn't be seeing
them again.

Afterward I decided Emma was right. It was a
waste for my grandmother, who still had the energy
of a much younger woman, to vegetate here. She
could get a companion for Grandpa. He probably
wouldn't know the difference. She could go to her
boards and do her charitable things and even travel
with her friends. It was a waste of life not to, but I
knew better than to tell her what I thought.

* * *

Soon after that my father appeared at the house late one afternoon. He had piloted someone to Miami and had one free evening before he had to take off again.

He finished a Scotch on the rocks and settled the affairs of the world with Grandmother in a leisurely discussion in which they both agreed that all politicians were either idiots or crooks or both. Then he asked me, "Want to go for a walk on the beach with me, Kelly?"

"I'd love to walk," I said.

A storm had cleared the air. The sky was a clean sweep of blue up and away to infinity, and scalloped waves foamed up against the shore.

"Want to run a little first?" he asked.

"Why not?" We were barefoot, but we tried it anyway. The wet sand gave comfortably under our feet. Out toward the horizon a three-masted sailing ship was keeping pace with us. It looked like something out of a history book on the early eighteen hundreds. Dad nodded when I pointed it out to him. Then he slowed down and so did I. It was time to talk.

"I've got good news for you," he said.

"That school in Albany accepted me?"

"Yes, that. They said they'd be glad to place you for the fall even though we applied late, but that isn't all. There's good news about your mother."

My heart stopped for a beat. I'd given up hoping for a change in her. "Tell me!" I demanded.

"Well, she's coming out of it. There's finally been a turnabout. They've got her on a medication that's working, and it looks as if she'll be able to go home instead of to another treatment center."

"Home! Oh, Dad, that's fabulous. Then I can go home too."

"No, honey. She's going to have a long convalescence."

"And I'll go home to help her."

"That's not—it wouldn't be wise. Your mother needs time to get back on her feet and we have to know—"

"Dad, stop treating me like a child. I can *help* Mother."

"Afraid not. It wouldn't be healthy for either of you. Her job is to get well. Yours is to grow up. You'll be leaving home in a few years. It's better if she doesn't get used to depending on you again."

"Who says?"

"The psychologist—your mother and I—we agree."

"You mean I'm still going to boarding school?"

"That's the plan."

"Well, how about going home weekends? Can I do that at least?"

"We'll see."

"See what?"

"How things go."

We veered higher up the sand to avoid an eagerly reaching wave that splashed us anyway. It was wonderful that Mother was getting better. What did I want? I wanted to touch her. I wanted to put my arms around her and hug her. I wanted that with a sudden fierce hunger that I hadn't known was in me. "I'm going to call her," I said.

"She's planning to call you tonight."

"But what will she do at home all by herself?"

"She has a lot to do. You don't realize how sick she's been. Just ordinary things like getting up and getting her own breakfast will be a challenge for a while."

"And then? I mean, when she's back to normal? What's to keep her from getting sick again?"

"Listen, Kelly, she's a bright woman. She knows she's got to fill up her life with something besides you. Maybe she'll go back to school. Dr. Landsberg is going to work on that with her as well as doing some diet and exercise therapy, and the psychiatrist says the medication should keep her on an even keel. So it'll be all right. You can stop worrying. She's not your problem."

There were clouds on the horizon now, tinged pink and lavender from the sunset we couldn't see over behind the rooftops of the houses lining the beach. Three pelicans flew in an uneven triangle. I saw one plummet, diving straight down into the water. It submerged and then rose dripping and flew off looking like an ancient pterodactyl, more reptile than bird. Evening always made me sad, but something more was wrong inside me tonight. I didn't know what. I was glad Mother was getting better, but I couldn't taste the joy of it somehow. I had the phone call to look forward to at least. Maybe all I needed was to hear her voice.

My father left after dinner. In the living room, I fiddled with the cedar-lined silver music box designed to hold the cigarettes no one smoked anymore. It played a Strauss waltz as I opened the cover and closed it, turning the music on and off over and over until Grandmother, who was sitting across from me near the fireplace, snapped, "Kelly, must you do that?"

"Sorry," I said and looked again at the clock on the mantlepiece next to the bronze horseman.

At eight the phone finally rang. I dashed to pick up the receiver.

"Mother?"

"Kelly, my darling! How are you?"

"How am *I*? I'm fine. How are you?"

"Great. Well, better, and that's great, isn't it?" She sounded excited, full of her old energy. "I think. We think. The doctors and I all think I'm really coming out of it."

"When do you leave the hospital?"

"Saturday."

"That's wonderful. Oh, Mother, that's the most wonderful news I've heard all summer. And will Dad stay home with you for a while?"

"Well, your father can only be here for the weekend, but that's okay. I can manage alone."

"Can you?"

"Sure, I'm a big girl now." The laugh was to show how ridiculous it was for me to worry.

"I guess that's a good thing," I said, "considering you've got a grown-up daughter. Listen, when do I see you?"

"Soon, my darling. Oh, very soon, I hope. I miss you so much. You can't believe how much I—" She stopped. "Let's not get mushy," she said. "You don't want me weeping all over the floor when I'm finally feeling up again."

"I'm supposed to go to boarding school in Albany this fall," I said.

"Yes, darling. Won't that be good? It's only half an hour away. We can talk on the phone and we can see each other."

"Mother, why do I have to go to boarding school? Wouldn't you rather I was home with you every night?"

"I don't think so. Your father and I talked, and we think—I feel, it's better for both you and me if—

oh, Kelly, I don't know for sure. I really don't know, but until I'm sure I've made it, I'm afraid—"

She sounded upset, as if my pushing her so hard was making her unsure. "Anyway," I said, "at least I'll be seeing you soon, right?"

"Right. Now tell me, has the summer been terrible for you, darling? Tell me the truth."

"A little dull," I said, "but not so bad. I wrote you about most of it."

"Yes, yes, I have all your beautiful letters. I've been reading them. For a while I was so out of it I couldn't—but now, I'm going to read them all over again. They deserve rereading, and darling, I appreciate that you kept writing even when I didn't write you back. It means so much to know—" Her voice broke. "I'm still shaky," she confessed. "Everything upsets me, even nice things."

"That's okay," I said. "I understand. It's like after you have a fever when you're still weak, isn't it?"

"A lot like that."

"Maybe you better lie down and rest now," I said. "But it's so great to hear your voice and I'm so glad you're getting better. Mother, I love you very much."

"I love you too, my angel, a whole bunch."

I had the receiver clenched so tightly in my fingers that it was hard to let go when we hung up. Still something nagged at me, and I couldn't put my finger on what it was. She was getting well. Why wasn't I overjoyed, plain and simple? But it wasn't simple.

Chapter 14

In bed that night I started thinking about Evan.
Love and support he had said. Would he have
survived and been such a super man without it?
Love and support—who was my mother going to
get it from if I went off to school and let her
struggle on her own? Dad, at best, was only going
to be home sporadically. Then what? What was she
going to do with herself in that big empty house
with nobody even to cook dinner for or talk to?
Surely no doctor would prefer her to live alone,
without me there. Grandmother's friends had said it
was a waste of her life to devote herself to Grandpa
now. Waste or not, it was what she wanted to do.
She couldn't leave Grandpa in a nursing home and
live her own life, not her. I sat up straight in bed.
The sea was pounding its way in and hissing out in
counterpoint with my breathing. I knew what had
been missing—something in me and now I'd found
it. I took a deep breath, feeling strong enough to lift

the world and make it turn for me. Then I went peacefully to sleep.

At breakfast I told Grandma, "I've decided not to go to boarding school after all. I'm going home to be with my mother."

"Really!" she said and set the teapot down. "You've decided, have you? I was under the impression you're still fourteen years old, not quite of an age to make adult decisions."

"Grandma, fourteen or not, I've thought about it, and I know you and my father are wrong. No way can I leave my mother to make it alone. I have to be there when she needs me . . ."

"Nonsense," Grandma picked up her teacup and sipped as if that one word concluded the discussion.

". . . Just the way you have to take care of Grandpa even though everyone tells you you shouldn't," I said.

"I am an old woman. You are a child and there's the difference."

"My age isn't as important as you think. I need to do that for my sake so I can like myself. I'm going to be home Saturday when she gets there."

"And how do you plan to get home? Walk?"

"If you won't buy me a plane ticket, I'll call Evan and ask him to lend me the money."

"Oh, you will, will you?" She looked at me with a glint of amusement in her eyes. "And what will your father say to all this?"

"Nothing. He'll understand."

"You don't know what you're talking about, my child," she said. "You are talking about sacrificing your life for your mother. At your age, when every new experience is essential for your development, you can't take on the burden of a sick, dependent woman. You have to concern yourself with realizing your own potential."

"I can help my mother and realize my potential too. I can do both. Don't worry, Grandma. I'm too self-centered to sacrifice too much."

"There's no point in my arguing with you. I'll call your father." Grandmother put down her teacup and went immediately to the phone.

I sat on the edge of my chair in the garden, tempting a small greenish bird who had flitted down from the palm tree to the breakfast table. It hopped to a dish, eyeing me, snatched a muffin crumb and flew away. My grandfather, who was still at the table, began to rise from his chair, pushing himself up with difficulty. "Ah, ah, ah," he said and couldn't shove the chair back to leave himself room to stand.

I took him gently by the arms and urged him back into his seat. "It's all right, Grandpa. She'll be back in a few minutes. You just sit down and wait a while." I stood beside him patting his arm the way Grandma did to reassure him. To my surprise, he responded by relaxing. I picked up the napkin he had dropped and wiped his chin clean of jam. I didn't do it easily. It cost me an effort, the kind of effort being there for my mother was going to cost me. For an instant I was scared. Could I really do what I'd determined to do?

Before I could answer my own question, my grandmother called me to the phone to speak to my father. While she stood in the open doorway watching me, I repeated much the same thing to him that I had said to her. His arguments duplicated Grandmother's, and my resolve hardened. Finally, I just begged, "Please, Dad. You've got to let me do this.

I just cannot go away to school and leave Mother to struggle alone. I can't *not* be there with her."

"I told you I'll be home."

"Not for long enough."

"Kelly, it wouldn't be good for you—"

"It's what I need to do," I said and held on to my certainty until I wore him out.

"Let me speak to your grandmother again," he finished wearily.

She had watched me. Now I stood and listened openly to her end of the conversation.

"No, I don't approve," she said. "Forcing her is not the question, but whether she can take so much on herself and still manage to live a normal life . . . Yes, of course, she means it. Yes, in my opinion . . . Yes, all right then, but first I'll call this Ph.D. psychologist you have such a high opinion of and see what she advises."

"What did you say yes to, Grandmother?" I asked when she hung up.

"Your father asked me if I thought you were strong enough."

"And you said, yes?"

"You're my granddaughter, Kelly, and an Allgood whether you want to be or not."

I fingered the seashell at my neck and hesitated. I wanted to say that I was glad to have some of her in me, that I had learned to admire a lot about her this summer, but I hadn't forgiven her for despising my mother. In the meantime, she had begun dialing again. I wondered if you could just call psychologists up in the middle of the day like that and have them be at their desks waiting to talk to you. Apparently, if you were Grandmother, you could.

Now it was her turn to explain briefly to Dr. Landsberg what I planned to do.

"She's only fourteen," Grandmother concluded before handing the receiver over to me. I took it and said hello.

"Yes," I said and steeled myself to resist.

"Your grandmother is concerned, and I think legitimately, that helping your mother could have negative effects on you."

"I don't see that at all."

"Well, while I agree that it might benefit your mother to have you home in this early part of her recovery, I do see some danger to you. That is, if you allow your mother to become dependent on you and feel responsible for keeping her company when you should be out socializing with your peers, that could stunt your emotional and social development."

"Not unless I let it," I said.

"Well, if you're determined and you do go home, remember this: You're her daughter, not her friend," Dr. Landsberg said, and I was jolted by this unexpected reminder of my uneasiness long ago when Mother sometimes boasted that I was her best friend. ". . . You could help her by encouraging her to do things in the community," Dr. Landsberg was saying. "You could be the mediator to help your mother make contacts for herself, to make friends of her own. That would be a good use of your energies. Your mother has to have her own life, not yours."

"I plan to go one seeing my friends and doing school things just like before," I said. "My mother wouldn't want me to give up my social life altogether. She's not selfish."

"I'm sure she'd never mean to be, but—"

"And if I'm home, even just part of the day," I said, "at least she'd have somebody there who loves her and she wouldn't be so alone. That's got to help."

"It should, but you must also realize you may not be able to help enough," Dr. Landsberg warned. "That is, she could have a relapse. It's possible she could even need to be hospitalized again, even with all of us doing our best to support her. Do you understand that? In the last analysis, your mother has to help herself, Kelly."

"I know that. I just want to be there rooting for her."

Dr. Landsberg laughed. "Well, then, I'd say your mother is lucky to have a daughter like you in her rooting section. . . . Let me talk to your grandmother again."

"I can go?" I asked when Grandmother finally hung up.

She sighed. "I suppose. But you must promise on your word of honor to tell us if it gets to be too much for you."

"It won't be too much."

"Perhaps not," Grandmother said. Then with a wistful smile she asked, "Do you think that you might return to visit with me sometime? You could bring a friend along to make it less dull for you here."

"I hope I can come back," I said.

"Another time we might start off on the right foot together and then—"

"Grandmother," I said lightly, "you know I'll be back. You're still six Scrabble games ahead of me."

She smiled at that and said, "Whatever you may

think of me, Kelly, I want you to know I'm very proud of you."

"I'm proud of you too," I said, unable to hold the words back any longer. After all, she couldn't help what she was, and maybe some day she'd learn to appreciate my mother.

Grandmother insisted on accompanying me in the taxi to the airport, but Grandpa had to go with us, and he kept trying to get out of the cab and asking where we were going, so in the end, she let me go into the terminal by myself. We kissed each other good-bye in the backseat of the taxi.

"Your father will be at the airport to take you home. You'll take care of yourself, won't you?"

"Of course," I said. "And you take care of yourself, Grandma. I'll let you know how it goes."

"If you need anything—"

"Don't worry," I said and waved and ran off into the terminal building after the cart on which my bags had been piled by the porter. She was quite a person, as Dad had said, and I was glad she was my grandmother, but I was on my way home and I had no patience for backward looks.

It was easy to travel alone. I just kept asking for directions and people were happy to give them. Before I knew it, we were in the air on a clear day in a half-empty plane. The pilot flew above the coastline. I watched the narrow piping of sand unwind along the eastern edge of the Carolinas and Chesapeake Bay and saw the complicated design of its vast shoreline. I saw large ships, their wakes like lines drawn in the sea behind them, and hills furred with dark green trees and the cross-hatching of streets and highways in the heavily industrial cities. I could almost feel what my father found so fascinating about flying, or maybe my elation was just because I was going home.

The skyscrapers of New York were tall and narrow as reeds, but it was annoying to have to land at Kennedy where we took on gas and a change of passengers. I didn't have to change planes, just wait impatiently until we were airborne again and then for another forty minutes before we set down with a thump at the Albany airport.

Behind the glass windows of the terminal building, I saw a crowd of people waiting to greet the passengers who were climbing down the the metal steps that had been wheeled to the plane. I saw my father's face and then my mother's so radiant with love for me that I was dazzled as I walked toward her. Her eyes were shining. Her hair was a jaunty cap to set off her tip-tilted nose and her smiling mouth. She was my mother again, a little thinner, but still herself, and in that instant I knew who the king of the sea was. He was anybody who loved you enough to be there for you when you needed him.

I flung myself into Mother's arms and squeezed her tightly while she hugged me. "My darling, my own, my child. I'm so happy to have you home!" she cried.

"Me too," I said. "I missed you, Mother, but I'm here now."

"Yes, you're here." We laughed then, and I hugged and kissed my father. Without letting go of each other, we all walked toward the baggage area talking about ordinary things, whether my suitcases would be first or last to arrive, and how long my hair had grown, and what we should do about dinner, and how we would celebrate being a family again. I saw no trace of a sad shell lady in Mother, but even if her happiness didn't last long, it would be all right. The king of the sea was there for her now. The king of the sea was me.

About The Author

Carole S. Adler was born in New York and attended Hunter College High School and Hunter College. She earned a master's degree in education from Russell Sage College, and for eight years taught English in a middle school in Niskayuna, New York, where she and her husband raised three sons and now live. She has had sixteen stories for teenagers published in magazines, and ten novels for young people have appeared to date, including THE SILVER COACH, DOWN BY THE RIVER and THE ONCE IN A WHILE HERO. THE MAGIC OF THE GLITS, her first published book, won the Golden Kite Award and the William Allen White Award.

Confronting the real issues in a realistic way...

JUNIPER BOOKS